ALICE BARKER

ON THE STROKE
OF TWELVE

ISBN: 9798566360201
Cover art by Alice Barker
Library of Congress Control Number: 2018675309
Printed in the United States of America

For my number one fans, the Liverpool ladies.
Thank you for all your support, and for waiting
so patiently.

CHAPTER ONE
CLARA

Snow fluttered down from the night sky, the icy formations looking like a dusting of sugar as they fell, sparkling, on the ground. Clara shivered and tugged her warm red woollen scarf further up her nose as she stepped onto the train platform.

Clara loved Christmas. Without doubt, it was her favourite time of the year. University had finished for the semester and now she was on her way home, the day before Christmas Eve, her suitcase dragging behind her and desperate to see her Mama and her younger brother, Ferdy.

Clara sighed irritably as she pushed all thoughts of cosy nights in front of the fire right out of her mind; she had a long train ride to go before she could even think about any of that, and by the time she got home, it would be very late and everyone would have already gone to sleep. Mind you, she couldn't wait to see them in the morning, catching up on the gossip and reminiscing about times gone by. Clara smiled despite her sullen mood. She really ought to be more cheerful; after all, it was Christmas!

Keeping this in mind, she turned away from the platform and went to go and get a drink from the nearby concessions stand. She had about ten minutes until her train arrived. Making it to the front of the queue, she paid for a warm cup of hot chocolate and sat down on a bench to sip at it, from where she would be able to see the train coming. As the soothing liquid slipped down her throat, Clara shivered pleasantly. Usually, she was more of a coffee drinker, but there was something about hot chocolate that was just so incredibly seasonal.

The obligatory few minutes passed, and before long the train pulled into the station. Clara stepped forward, and, anticipating the mandatory hustle and bustle that went hand-in-hand with boarding trains, held her drink aloft so that she didn't accidentally spill it.

She pushed to the front of the crowd, and in turn, people barged past her. It wasn't long though before she was stood in the doorway of the train carriage and eyeing up which seat to take. She was just starting to head to the empty back row when a burly businessman in a very official-looking suit jostled her elbow – and spilt her festive cup of cocoa all down the front of her nice new white knitted jumper, not even stopping to apologise as he left the carriage.

Clara harrumphed indignantly, irritated by the sticky brown droplets that were now dripping down her sweater. Then she sighed, resigned, and sunk heavily into a seat.

She couldn't wait to get out of the city. University had its perks, like being finally being able to study Geography at an educational institution that was world-renowned for it, but the people who lived in the town it occupied always seemed to be rushed and rude with little regard for others. This did not sit well with Clara, who, despite her high social status, had always done her best to try and be kind and compassionate.

Settling down for the journey home, she put her now-empty cup on the table before her and pulled out her phone, putting her earpieces in. She scrolled through her music library, deciding what to listen to, and finally plumped for some classical; the melodies were heavenly, and besides, it reminded her of happier times.

With nothing else to do, she came out of the music app and opened her social media feed. Instantly, she was inundated by images of the end-of-term festivities she'd left behind at the university; loud, raucous parties where people drank alcohol and spirits, their designer clothes all rumpled as the children of the country's upper-class frivolously squandered their parents' money in a wanton display of wealth. Clara sighed. She might be a Stahlbaum, but it had never occurred to her to act in such a way. Yes, a lot of the families of the pupils who studied at her university were well-off, but the truth was that their fortunes were relatively new, and so their parents – bankers, lawyers, entrepreneurs and the like – were hopelessly indulgent. The

Stahlbaums, however, were a different creed; they were descended from German aristocracy, and they were proud of their name, with some of Clara's ancestors having held titles at foreign courts and shares in shipping companies before making their fame and fortune by getting involved with rail at the height of the Industrial Revolution. She was sure there had even been a distant connection to Prince Albert somewhere. Clara couldn't grasp all the details, no matter how many times her father had shown her the Stahlbaum family tree whilst he was still alive. However, she did know that her family's pictures often ended up inside glossy magazines, that not everyone lived in a nineteenth-century mansion, and that simply stating her surname often made people fall over themselves in an attempt to please her. Her mother was always attending or hosting some fabulous event, champagne was always freshly poured, and neither she, nor her little brother, had ever wanted for anything growing up.

Clara was truly grateful for what she had. She knew she was more fortunate than most. Actually, if it was up to her, she would forgo the Stahlbaum name altogether, adopting a simpler moniker like Robinson or Ford, and slip into obscurity. As long as she could see some of the world, she was happy. She didn't need anything else.

As she scanned her social media feed, full of the opulent revellers, she grimaced. Elite universities for rich kids were all good and well, but a little humility certainly wouldn't go amiss amongst a great many of the students. Maybe that was why she didn't have many friends; she refused to be snobbish and gloat with the rest of them.

Still, it didn't matter now; they were all gone for a fortnight, and this Christmas break would be the last chance at peace she'd have before exam stress well and truly kicked in next semester.

The train carriage was warm and snug as it continued on the south-bound journey that would eventually deliver Clara home. She yawned. Only another four hours to go. Forgetting all thoughts of university, the city and spoilt students, Clara closed her eyes and fell asleep.

CHAPTER TWO
SWEETMEADOW
PLACE

As the train ground to a stop outside a station that was little more than a dot on the line, Clara awoke, then seeing where she was, picked up her bags and hurriedly dashed to the doors before they closed on her. Making it just in time, she thanked the conductor and stepped out into the cold. After a few more moments the train pulled away and sped off, swallowed up by the night as it continued on its journey.

Clara was all alone as she stood on the platform; the snow was still falling and it piled in little drifts around her feet. A nearby clock told her it was coming up to 11:00pm as she gathered herself and headed inside the station.

It was deserted except for a cleaner and a very weary-looking ticket officer, who rested his chin on his hand as he sat in his booth and tried desperately not to doze off. The snow had made the air still and quiet, and as Clara took a seat and called a local taxi rank, she felt almost exposed. Before too long however, the car arrived and she jumped in the back, trying to ignore the driver's shocked expression when she

told him she wanted to go to Sweetmeadow
Place.

Her mother, as worried and well-meaning
as she was, had offered to send Pyotr, their
butler, to pick her up in the Rolls, but Clara had
gently declined. The thought of getting the poor
man out of bed at such a ridiculous hour to
come and pick her up on such an awfully wintry
night flew in the face of everything that she
stood for.

It was a forty-five minute drive from the
station to Sweetmeadow Place, and with a sense
of regret Clara wished that she had travelled
home earlier, during in the day, for now she
could not see the wide, open countryside fields
of her childhood. It didn't matter to Clara that

they would have been snow-covered rather than their summery lush green; she was so grateful to be out of the claustrophobic city that right now she'd be thankful for any kind of open space, no matter how it presented itself. In the morning, she decided, she would see if Ferdy wanted to join her for a snowball fight in the grounds, playing like they had done when they were little.

Before long, gravel crunched under the taxi's tyres. In the glare of the headlights, Clara could only see a few inches in front of her – the long pathway, the tall fir trees that lined either side of it, and the heavily-falling snow splattering softly onto the windscreen – but she knew she had made it home. She felt it in her bones. She didn't even react to the house as it appeared in front of them, even though the taxi driver's eyes were agog as he came to a stop on the forecourt.

Clara dug in her purse and pulled out the correct fare, plus a little extra. "Here you go." she told him. "Keep the change." He thanked her profusely as she declined his offer of help with the luggage and clambered out. What was the point in having access to a fortune if you didn't share at least some of it with others, especially at Christmas?

Clara bounced her suitcase up the ten stone steps at the front of the house, having become well practiced over the years, and fumbled for her key in her coat pocket before opening one side of the antique double doors and letting herself in, as quiet as a church mouse.

The grand hallway, with its sweeping double staircase, was empty, the only sound being that of the ancient grandfather clock in the corner, that was emitting its deep ticking as the pendulum swung. Not wanting to wake anyone, Clara carefully deposited her bags at the foot of the staircase, laying them down on the polished white marble floor. She was too tired to change for bed now anyway; she would get her things in the morning. Undoing her laces, she stepped out of her boots and left them there too, then hotfooted it upstairs to find her childhood bedroom.

The doors on the upper floor of Sweetmeadow Place stood uniformly either side of a long walkway, but Clara knew that opening them would only lead to more rooms within rooms. For here, no one simply had mere bedrooms but more their own miniature apartments, with en suite bathrooms, dressing rooms and great, impressive beds, with high plastered ceilings painted in tasteful white and soft furnishings made from luxury fabrics. Even Pyotr had a small wing to himself.

As a baby, Clara had slept and played in a pretty pink nursery designed by her mother, with all the trappings and trimmings a future debutante could ever need, filled with frills and lace and pearls, but as the years went by, Clara had begun to grow into her own person. She'd climbed trees down by the river with the local boys, took great delight in milking the cows and collecting eggs from the hens that resided here on the family's land, and studied maps – things her mother had said were not suitable activities for a young lady. Clara knew, even from being a girl, that she had no intention of being a stereotypical Stahlbaum.

Reaching the end of the hallway, Clara opened a narrow door that was positioned in the far corner. Behind it was a small stairwell, which was built into the original foundations of the house. The stairs too were just as old, shaped in a tight spiral that rounded a corner. Clara had found it one day whilst she was playing hide and seek with Ferdy, and once she saw what was at the top of it, she had claimed the space as her own, and on her ninth birthday, she had requested that it be made into a bedroom for her. Her parents had surprisingly agreed.

Bracing herself against the cold breeze that drifted out from the opening, Clara turned on the light switch at the bottom of the stairs and ascended, a warm glow beckoning her from above. She rounded the tight cranny, and when she reached the upper landing, she grinned. Now, she was truly home.

The Nook, as she had taken to calling it, was exactly as she'd left it. Her double bed was neatly made, its homemade pink-and-green patchwork quilt draped invitingly over it. Fairy lights were threaded through the beams above the headboard, weaving their way into the alcoves of the tiny attic room. The walls were painted a warm sage green, whilst fluffy rugs in co-ordinating shades of pink and cream warmed the bare wooden floorboards. A work desk stood on one side of the room, with a window seat overlooking the rose garden on the other; if Clara had climbed onto the cushions in daylight, she would have been able to see the pretty blooms. Girlish paraphernalia was everywhere; pastel watercolour paintings of ballerinas and silken slippers hung on the walls, a groaning bookshelf containing teen romance novels stood in another corner, and stuffed animals languished atop the armoire at the foot of the bed, discarded and forgotten.

Clara tiptoed across the floor and opened another door that was directly opposite her.

Inside was a tiny en-suite bathroom, consisting of a toilet, sink and shower cubicle. She went to relieve herself, desperate after the long train ride, and washed her hands.

When she'd finished, she returned to the bedroom and pulled off her scarf and her jumper, laying them neatly folded on the chair at the work desk; she would put the dirty jumper in the laundry tomorrow. Then she turned off the lights via the switch on the wall and dove under the covers, pulling them up to her chin. She was fast asleep in seconds.

Sometime later, Clara was awoken by the sound of birdsong drifting in from outside. She turned to face the window and was surprised to see bright sunlight streaming in. She lay in bed staring at the ceiling for a few minutes, lost in her own thoughts, and then swung her feet out onto the floor before heading across to the window seat.

Using the sleeve of her t-shirt to wipe away the condensation, she looked down over the garden. The snow had ceased to fall, and the sky was now a beautiful, clear glacier blue. Weak sunlight danced through the branches of the bare trees, casting amber flecks across the white snow that covered everything Clara could see, from the last of the wilting rose heads to the line of the faraway forest that demarked the end of the Sthalbaum's land.

A movement on the edge of the lawn caught Clara's eye, and she smiled as she saw her mother, in a thick woollen coat, pottering about in her vegetable patch just beyond the roses. Clara watched, and then, as the elder woman straightened up and looked back towards the house, waved. Mama's face broke into a wide grin, and she headed inside.

Clara gasped happily and dashed away from the window. She barrelled down the entrance to The Nook, charged down the hallway and took the grand staircase steps two at a time. She could hear her mother calling her before she'd even entered the kitchen at the back of the house, and so she ran and ran and did not stop until she was enfolded, laughing and giggling, into her embrace.

"Clara, Clara, Clara! It is so good to have you home." Mama kissed the top of her head. "Let me look at you." She held her daughter at arm's length and took in her stale shirt and rumpled leggings. "Why, you looked so dishevelled!"

"I slept in my clothes last night. I didn't want to wake anyone." Clara explained as she recovered herself.

"Silly thing! I saw your bags at the bottom of the stairs. You should have got Pyotr to bring them up for you." She was hollering out of the kitchen doorway for the butler before anyone could stop her.

Almost immediately, a middle-aged man with a shock of white swept-back hair entered the room. He was wearing a smart dark suit and looked quite exasperated. "Madam called?" he asked politely, his heavy German accent flavouring the hint of weariness that crept into his voice.

"Miss Clara is awake now." Mama informed him in bossy, business-like tones – unnecessarily, since he could see that Clara was standing right next to her. "Take her bags upstairs please."

"Of course." he agreed brusquely. Then he turned to Clara and his face softened as he smiled at her. "*Guten morgen*, Miss Clara."

"*Guten morgen*, Pyotr." said Clara happily, slipping easily into the German he had taught her. "*Wie geht's dir?*"

Pyotr let nothing in his face slip as he said: "*Ich bin gestresst.*" Then he gave her a slight nod and left the room.

As soon as he had gone Clara rounded on her mother. "There was no need to do that." she said as she pulled out a chair at the worn kitchen table and sat down. "I could have carried them up myself later."

Her mother shrugged. "That's what we pay him for though, darling. Come on; let me make you some tea. You look wretched."

Behind her mother's back, Clara rolled her eyes. Mary Stahlbaum, previously Mary Collins, played the part of the aristocratic widow wonderfully well. Her parents, Clara's grandparents, had been fairly wealthy themselves; young Mary had studied at private school, gone on exotic holidays, ridden a pony, all that sort of thing. She had been a pretty twenty-one-year-old when she had met the darkly dashing Nicklaus and her life had changed forever. They had fallen in love, and in that love he had left her his estates, fortune and legacy. Now, eight years after his death, Mary took it upon herself to make sure the Stahlbaum name thrived and stayed true to its roots, ensuring there was no criticism or cross words from the many high-ranking cousins that still resided and thrived in their native Germany.

As the kettle boiled, Clara looked around the rustic country-style kitchen, the winter sun refracting off the terracotta-red walls and the stone fireplace that was still dusty with soot from the previous night's kindling. She'd always thought the house beautiful, but now that her father wasn't there to fill it, it always seemed just a bit too big.

Mama sat down in the seat across from Clara and slid her a mug of hot tea."How are things at university?" she asked as she took a sip of her own beverage.

"Okay. I'll have to do some revision while I'm here though. The tutors are really going to be pushing us next semester."

"That wasn't what I meant, and well you know it. What parties have you been to? How are your friends?"

Clara cringed. Her socialite mother would be aghast if she knew the truth; that her only daughter was a recluse and a loner. "There haven't been any parties, Mama; we've been studying, like I said." The lie came quickly and easily. There had been parties, of course. She just hadn't been invited.

"I see. And what about that handsome young man you were seeing? Jeremy, John..."

"James." Clara corrected. "It's over. He ended it." Her facial expression became pained. Truthfully, she had ended it, after she had found him kissing some other girl in the faculty library, but it was still new, it hurt, and she didn't want to go through all the details with her busybody mother, at least not yet; that would have meant having to relive it.

Mary's face became one of full sympathy. "Oh Clara, I'm so sorry. I could tell you were smitten."

Despite herself, Clara heard her voice tremble as she asked: "What's wrong with me, Mama?"

"Nothing, my love, absolutely nothing. You're as stunning and as beautiful as Christmas itself. Try not to be so down, dear. Tomorrow night we'll have you all dolled up and you'll shine up bright like a new penny."

That made Clara start. "Tomorrow night?"

"Yes. Didn't I say? We're having a little Christmas party. A few friends, a bit of fizz, maybe a few eligible bachelors..."

"Oh no." Clara put her head in her hands. No wonder Pyotr had said he was stressed earlier.

"What? Oh darling, don't be like that. It's Christmas Eve!"

"I didn't bring any decent clothes!"

"We'll find you something. Do you really think five-hundred-years' worth of German heritage is going to let you down when you can't find an outfit for a last minute engagement?" Mama winked at her as she stood up and walked away.

"Mama, what does that mean? There better not be some old heirloom dress stuffed up there in the attic! Mama... Mama!"

But Mary had gone. She wasn't listening, instead humming away to herself and probably deciding what toppings to put on the many trays of canapés she would no doubt serve. Clara groaned. So much for a relaxing Christmas.

At that exact moment the back door banged open, sending small flurries of snow into the kitchen and making the air cold. Clara looked up as the figure in the entryway pulled off its bobble hat and unwound its scarf from its insulated face.

"Whoops! Sorry Sis. I didn't want to go out today, but the sheep needed seeing to."

"Ferdy!" Clara cried, and she sprung up from the table and wrapped her arms around her baby brother's neck.

"Well, good morning to you too." he chuckled.

Ferdy, short for Ferdinand, was arguably Clara's most favourite person in the whole world. Sixteen years old and with shoulders that would make an ox blush, he was a large lad, with a build designed for lifting and carrying heavy things. This was because Ferdy had been romping about the Stahlbaum fields since he was a cheeky toddler with a keen taste for blackberries. He had a mop of fair hair and a farmer's tan, even in winter, with a smile that broke into a bright grin for pretty much anyone who treated him well. Unlike Clara, he enjoyed the aristocratic lifestyle. He had no desire to see the world, and it was fully expected, by him and everybody else, that he should do nothing except marry a good honest country girl and oversee the running of Sweetmeadow Place until he was no longer able to.

The very idea of such an existence bored Clara to tears; she longed for adventure and far-off destinations. She had to hand it to Ferdy though; he had an innate way with the Place, knowing the landscape and livestock by heart. He also had a solid dream and a solid plan; something that she had yet to achieve despite the two years she'd spent at university, and she envied him slightly for it.

Still in his outerwear, Ferdy meandered over to the kettle and made himself a cup of tea with the last of the hot water.

"Did you know Mama's hosting a Christmas party tomorrow night?" Clara asked him.

Ferdy tipped his head back and let out a great big belly laugh. "Did I know? She's only been planning it for about three months."

"Oh dear God."

"Hey now, be kind to her. It's the only thing she's got going for her since Papa died."

Clara smiled upon hearing her father's pet name. Even after they were fully grown and could speak properly, he had always insisted on them calling him Papa.

"You still really miss him, don't you?"
Ferdy asked gently. "I do too. Christmas was his
favourite time of year... which means it's the
worst time of year for Mama, now. That's why
she throws parties. Not because she's vain but
because it helps her get through it. That's why
we have to put on a brave face. For her."

Clara blinked. She had never thought
about it like that before.

Ferdy continued. "She cries more now
that you're gone. I think that she feels like she's
lost her daughter too, bless her." A sly grin
formed on his face.

"That's just blackmail Ferdy. Okay, fine. I
promise you I'll smile at least once during the
party."

"That's my introverted anti-social sister!" cried Ferdy cheekily, and before Clara could swat him, he left the room.

CHAPTER THREE
AN UNEXPECTED GUEST

Clara stood by her bed, her hands on her hips, glaring ruefully at the dusky pink parcel that was folded neatly on top of her covers. She could hear the Christmas party in full swing downstairs, but so far she hadn't mustered up the courage to even get ready, partly because of what her mother had deemed fit for her to wear.

Clara hadn't even looked at it properly yet, but she already knew she hated it.

Sighing, Clara took the dress and held it at arms' length as it unfurled itself. She scowled. It had a lacy, off-the-shoulder bodice, and the skirts were made from tulle, stopping just above the ankle. The dress was the exact colour of sugarplums, with floral details picked out in lilac embroidery. Pretty – if you were a character in a Charles Dickens novel, that is.

But it wasn't like she had anything else to wear, and so she put it on, despite the fact that she felt as if she should have been wearing a corset underneath it. She was surprised to discover it fit her well, accentuating all the right places and yet not itching in anywhere inappropriate. Satisfied, she slipped on the matching flat pumps her mother had left for her by her bed, then looked at herself in the mirror above her desk and started fussing with her hair.

Her mother loved her hair, calling it the colour of spiced sherry, but not having time for frippery Clara never quite knew what to do with it; she could never style it in the elaborate ways she had seen in magazines and on celebrities. Still, tonight was about pleasing her mother, so she decided to try, doing a simple half up, half down style, curling a section of her hair into an elegant little chignon at the nape of her neck. Once done, she looked at herself in the mirror again. It would suffice. Actually, truth be told she rather liked the way the loose section of her dark hair accentuated her pale skin, with the majority of it falling down the side of her neck.

Next, she opened her makeup bag and started applying her cosmetics. She did her eye shadow, blending out the shimmering natural colours in the palette onto her lids. Mascara was next, and then blusher and lipstick. She applied some of her rose-scented perfume to her wrists, hair and neck, and then, in a moment of madness, added a quick drop to her décolletage. All done, she sat back and admired her handiwork.

When she saw who was looking back at her in the mirror, Clara was quite pleased. She certainly wasn't going to flaunt her looks and peacock around the house tonight – as no doubt the other young ladies in attendance were going to do – but her Mama was right; she had shined up brightly. Instead of looking pasty and tired, as she so often had in recent months, she came across as polished and graceful. Her eyes, so deep a brown they were almost black, twinkled in the ambient lighting, the secrets within them glittering like stars.

Clara hated to admit it, but now she had the dress on and all the components had come together, she rather liked her appearance. True, she never wanted to be a wealthy high society darling, but now, here, in her family's seat with the spirit of Christmas in the air, things felt different. The world outside of Sweetmeadow Place was unknowing that the Stahlbaums were about to do what they always did best; it was uninvited, and tonight, Clara was a lady in her own court. She smiled at her reflection.

And that was when she heard the noise.

It was a strange noise, like a soft scratching, as if someone was whispering and trying, unsuccessfully, to go unheard. It grew a little louder, and a little louder again, until it seemed to be coming from the skirting board right by the edge of Clara's bed. Perturbed, she slowly turned her head and looked in the direction of the sound.

There, standing on its hind legs and gazing at her with a curiosity that did not befit it, was a little brown mouse.

Clara froze like a statue. She was not afraid of mice, but she did not want to startle the little fellow either. Instead, she simply looked at the mouse, and he looked at her, his whiskers twitching and his head on one side as if she was of great interest to him. Time seemed to stand still as they regarded each other. Clara felt the slightest hint of a knowing smile curving up her lips as she did so.

"Mistress Clara! Your mama calls for you!"

The shout from Pyotr at the bottom of The Nook's stairs made both the human and the mouse jump in surprise. Clara could only watch as her newfound – albeit very small – friend bolted and clambered up into the rafters, squeezing through a tiny crack in the wall and then vanishing. Clara did her best to hide her frustration as she shouted back: "I'm coming, Pyotr."

She rose from her stool, making sure not to trip over her uncharacteristically long skirts as she did so. As she headed down the stairs however, the mouse was still on her mind. Despite the intelligent gaze he had set upon her, there was also something else strange about him, something she had forgotten in the absurdity of the moment but remembered now, and now she had it baffled her even further and led her to think, that, maybe, she had accidentally fallen asleep and simply dreamt the whole encounter.

The tiny little mouse had been wearing a red waistcoat.

CHAPTER FOUR
GIFTS AND GRIEF

Clara felt her feet become unsteady on the steps, and as her balance began to fail her she reached for the banister. Mice? Wearing waistcoats? That couldn't be true. That was silly, like something out of a fairy story told to wide-eyed children.

And yet... she had seen the mouse with her own eyes as he looked into hers in a way that was so bright it was unsettling. She had definitely seen him, she was certain of it.

There was just no logical reason to explain why the mouse should have been wearing a red waistcoat.

Catching her breath, she refocused as she heard the familiar tunes of the timeless Christmas carols floating up to her from downstairs. Of course; her mother's Christmas Eve party. That was what she had to concentrate on now, that was what was important. Not a half-dreamt dream about waistcoat-wearing mice.

Trying to compose her features into the picture of grace and elegance she had felt in her room, she headed to the grand staircase. Then, as she saw the scene that awaited her, she gasped.

The entrance hall, which had been so silent and empty only last night when she had snuck in, was now thronging with people, the majority of whom Clara did not know. They spilled out into the other rooms of the house; ladies in various states of formal dress chatted amiably to their acquaintances and sipped at sparkling wine whilst their husbands shifted at their elbows and looked decidedly uncomfortable. There were younger people, similar in age to herself, but Clara could tell, even just by hearing the echoes of their conversation, that they were made from the exact same mould as the students she had left behind in the city. The girls, all heavily made up, tossed their hair and fluttered their eyelashes as if never a thought went through their pretty little heads. Idiotically, the boys gawped over them, nudging their companions and whispering undoubtedly misogynistic comments to each other before bursting out into fits of raucous laughter. From her vantage point, Clara could see it all, and she hated it all.

Then suddenly, she saw something that shook her even further.

Ferdy, her little brother Ferdy, was one of those young men. There he stood, in a crisp white shirt, glass in hand, joking bawdily with the others and eyeing the young ladies admiringly alongside them. As Clara saw him look a particularly stunning beauty up and down, she felt her anger rise. How could her brother – her little brother! – partake in such a repulsive activity? She had half a mind to march down the stairs and pull him to one side for a word about his behaviour, but then at the last moment a horrible realisation hit her and she bit her tongue.

Those boys were Ferdy's friends. Those were the boys he spoke to in the evenings, who he hung around with at school, who he texted and called and played video games with. That group was his world – a world she had left behind when she'd set off for university. He was a teenager now, not the child who had hung on her every word, followed her everywhere, and sobbed alongside her in the privacy of their playroom after their father had passed away.

That baby brother was gone; Ferdy had learnt how to survive in her absence and though she was loathe to admit it, that thought made Clara quite sad and regretful.

Not wanting him to see her and the fact that she had broken her promise to be cheerful, Clara rushed down the stairs, taking care to hide her face so that no one could look upon the unshed tears that threatened to spill down her cheeks. Though she caught a fleeting glimpse of some of her mother's friends, no one called out to her or asked her why she fled. Everyone was here... but there was no one here for Clara.

Just at that moment someone barred her way.

"Ah, Clara! There you are! Where have you been?" It was her mother, whose face was flushed and whose glass of champagne wobbled in her hand as she spoke, threatening to spill it all down her red, sequinned dress. "My sweet, sweet Clara. Be a dear, will you, and go and dance for the guests in the dining room."

"What?" Clara was so stunned she began to think she had misheard.

"Clara, you're such a beautiful ballet dancer!"

Not any more, thought Clara. *Not since that day, and not ever again.*

"No." she told her mother curtly, and tried to get past her in order to continue her escape.

"Darling! I'm not asking much!" Mama slurred. "Just give them a twirl!"

Without waiting for her daughter's answer, she grabbed her by the arm and dragged her towards where the guests were waiting.

"Mama, I'm not – Mama, stop! Please!"

"You do protest too much, sweetheart!"

"But I can't dance! Not anymore! I –"

"Of course you can!" Ungracefully, Mama nudged the door of the dining room open. "Here she is, ladies and gentlemen! My Clara, ready to perform for you all."

There was polite applause as Clara reluctantly gauged her audience. They were all sat around the long dining room table, dressed in the same formal garb as all the other guests, and there was barely enough room to do a simple *ronde de jambe*, let alone a pirouette or anything else fancy.

Nevertheless, her mother pushed her into a space at the head of the table that was just about wide enough for Clara to stretch her legs, and pressed play on a nearby stereo.

Upon hearing the music, Clara's heart began to race. *No! Not that, Mama! Anything but that!*

Her stomach began to curdle and her palms started sweating as she began to hyperventilate; if she didn't calm herself she would have a full-blown panic attack. Memories that she had long since locked away flashed in her mind, and they sickened her.

Her audience waited expectantly. Clara looked at them blankly. She'd have to do something, but she'd had no time to rehearse, she had no partner and very little room. There was no way she could launch into a choreographed routine here. She would have to improvise. She would have to make it up. She would never forgive her mother for doing this. She would look like a fool. She –

She was thinking like a dancer.

As if her body had a mind of its own, she began to remember the graceful, beautiful steps. She started in first position, and then did a *plié*. Then the *ronde de jambe*. Then, using one of her mother's dining chairs as a makeshift *barre*, she gently arched into an *arabesque*, surprising herself by just how easily she could straighten her leg behind her and how pointed her toes were. She gradually lowered herself back down and went into fifth position before looking at the faces of her audience. They were rapt now, watching her intently, and Clara was wholly aware that she was beaming and flushed. What next? Was there room to do a couple of *fouétte* turns? It didn't matter, Clara decided. She would make room.

And so she launched into the *fouéttes*. She spun, one, two, three times, one foot never leaving the ground and the other foot folded neatly underneath her, which flared out slightly whenever she rotated. It was only her dining room, but for Clara, who hadn't danced for so long in so many years, it could just have easily have been The Royal Opera House or a Broadway stage. She was dancing, she was flying, and suddenly her soul was flying too, seizing the new chance at happiness she gave it and holding on to it tightly before it could be taken away again.

So caught up in this feeling was she that she had forgotten to take any notice of her *fouéttes* altogether. As she did another fast and fluid spin, the foot stabilising her arched, and she tripped and fell, headlong, into the table.

There were gasps as she came crashing down, and for a moment, Clara, dazed and confused, struggled to get up. When she did, however, everything came flooding back to her and she felt nothing but a tidal wave of embarrassment. She had just committed the biggest *faux pas* a ballerina could ever commit. She was not an elegant swan; she was instead a waddling goose, ungainly and clumsy and not much liked by anybody.

Clara looked around the room and saw the horrified faces of the guests staring back at her. Without saying another word, she bolted.

Clara's anger burned brighter than any of the Christmas candles that shone around the hallways as she ran, going to the only safe space she had left. To everyone else, Sweetmeadow Place was just an old, grand house, but to her it was her childhood home, her father's home, and she knew her way around it like the back of her hand.

Her father's study hadn't been redecorated in the years since he'd passed. Mama had her own reading room, and while she worked and did what was necessary to retain the Place, she was not master of the house in the way that Nicklaus Stahlbaum had been, in the way that his son Ferdinand would soon grow to be. It had been left, therefore, as an in-house monument to a beloved husband and Papa gone far too soon. No one questioned their decision. Pyotr might have run a duster around it once or twice a month, but beyond that, the room was left completely undisturbed.

Which was why, for Clara, it had become something of a sanctuary.

She lurched, sobbing and blind with emotion, through the door. The dark panelling and plush carpets enveloped her immediately as she staggered, unheeding, past the mahogany desk to the drinks cabinet that took up the entirety of the back wall. It felt like some sort of sacrilege, barging in on the place that had once belonged to her father with the intention of consuming his personal spirits, yet right now she did not care. Her father, her Papa, was not here, and so any attempt to try and preserve his existence was a sham. He was gone, and never again would he walk through the house with his gentleman's air, stooping down to pick Clara up before he swung her around and made her all the promises in the world.

The tears in her eyes were flowing freely now, hot and bitter. Clara flung open the door of the drinks cabinet and grabbed a heavy bottle of malt whisky from the bottom shelf. With shaking hands she poured some of the amber liquid into the nearby scotch glass that stood at the bottle's base, then picked it up and knocked the measure back. The whisky was scalding, too warm and sharp for Clara's taste, but it was strong and unforgiving, which was exactly what she needed. Pouring herself another glass, she turned around and gazed at the oil painting of her father that hung on the opposite wall above the great bureau, where he had written his letters and read trade reports.

Her father was handsome, with a beauty that had long been forgotten by the rest of the world. He had dark eyes that reminded Clara uncannily of her own, black hair that shone with a natural gloss that was evident even in the oils, and a handlebar moustache and beard that very nearly hid the curled-up corners of a mirthful smile that lightened his whole face.

Clara had photographs of him of course, including several on her phone that she had taken during spontaneous, carefree moments, but she loved this painting more than anything else. It made him look regal, loving, and proud. It elevated him to the status of the idol that he was in Clara's heart.

Yet he had gone now, just as Mama and Ferdy had gone too. Even Clara, when she looked at herself in the mirror, was reminded that she was no longer her Papa's little girl. She could no longer return to those memories, go back to a time where life had been easier and she had never known sorrow. The world kept on spinning, moving her further and further away from everything she loved, and now it was spinning too fast for Clara to catch up.

Heavily, she sat down in the chair at her father's desk and spoke aloud to the image on the wall above her.

"I told Ferdy I missed you, but that's not true. I need you, back here with me, with us." She swallowed a snivel as she quietly continued.

"I don't know who I am, Papa. I don't know where I fit, or what I'm supposed to do. If only you could tell me."

"Personally, I think you're doing a grand job."

Clara jumped out of her skin as the voice came from behind her. She turned to the door and saw a man, as ancient as dust motes, enter the room. He was hunched over a wooden cane, his back stooped and his salt-and-pepper hair thinning, but he was wearing a smart black frock coat and his eyes held a spark that had not yet gone out.

"Uncle Drosselmeyer!" Clara gasped, and she hurried to offer the unsteady man her elbow and lower him into the chair.

He sighed in relief as his aching back came to rest against the cushions of Nicklaus's old Chesterfield. "Thank you child. God bless you for having a kind heart even when you are grieving yourself."

"You heard all that?" Clara asked as she felt her face colour.

"Oh yes. But don't fret, my dear. You know I have never fit in well with this family myself. You have only ever been the one who truly saw me for what I am, especially after my beloved nephew died."

It was true. Ever since she was a young girl she had respected Uncle Drosselmeyer deeply, despite everyone else's attempts to cast him off as an eccentric old fool. Clara had to agree that there was something not quite conventional about him, but it was magical and mysterious, not threatening or dark. Uncle Drosselmeyer was obsessed with physics, chemistry and astrology, and was an ambassador for all things old; he remembered a time of courteousness and propriety, and he loved Germany. In fact, he felt so strongly about his homeland that he never would have left it had his treasured nephew not begged him to come to England so that he and his wife could take care of him as he got older and more infirm. Despite his strange ways, Clara tended to put others' opinions aside and follow her own instincts, and her great-uncle had never given her any reason not to trust him, so she did.

He spoke to her softly. "Whatever is troubling you child, you can tell me. I will repeat it to no one."

Clara struggled for a moment before easing her conscience. "I came home a few days ago, and in that time, I've realised how much everything has changed, and will continue to change. Ferdy is a grown man now, Mama is a socialite, and yet... I still think about Papa. And the more this continues, the more he disappears, and I don't want him to go."

Drosselmeyer grinned crookedly at her. "That is your German blood talking."

"It's impossible, I know, but I don't want to move on." She suddenly found the fire inside her soul raging hotly again, so strongly she could barely contain it. "I don't want any of this! I never asked for it!" She stood up, filled with fury now, impossible fury that was indeed fiery, but also icy, and it surged through her veins and made her feel indomitable and powerful beyond all measure. Suddenly she felt the words she needed to say, that she needed to use to get this feeling out of her, rush, unbidden, onto her tongue.

"Into time's embrace I wish to delve, and make the clocks stop at the stroke of twelve!"

She heard something then, like the final funereal note of a tolling bell intermingled with the cracking and creaking of breaking ice. Clara blinked and shook her head as if she had awoken from a trance. What on Earth had that been?

Something felt irrevocably changed inside of her, as if she had released something; something she knew but could not yet name, something she simultaneously felt confused, awed and terrified by.

She turned back to the Chesterfield, where her great-uncle Drosselmeyer was gazing at her as if she had just serenaded him with a delightful song or recited a particularly beautiful piece of poetry.

"I can smell it." his aged voice croaked. "Yes, I can definitely smell it. There is magic in the air this night."

Clara sank to her knees in front of him, taking his hands in hers. "Uncle... I don't know what that was, but it certainly wasn't –"

"*Meine güte*, Clara! Have you forgotten the date? It's Christmas Eve! Anything could happen!"

Clara couldn't meet his eyes. The last few moments had left her perplexed and stunned.

If Uncle Drosselmeyer saw her uncertainty, he took no notice of it. Instead, he held a long bony finger up in front of Clara's face. "I have a surprise for you." he intoned as he reached inside his jacket. He pulled out a tall, slightly thin parcel. "Consider it a Christmas gift."

Clara looked from the parcel to her uncle and back again, and when he motioned for her to take it, she pulled off the red ribbon and the golden paper and looked to see what was inside.

When she did see what it was, however, Clara tried not to recoil. It was a nutcracker; one of those classical European types with fluffy white hair, bared, gritted teeth and scarlet, pulled-back lips. The painted eyes on the figure were vacant as they stared at Clara, and yet somehow she felt as if they knew her every thought. She tried her best to repress a shudder. She had seen these often at Christmas markets and had always found herself creeped out by them. She couldn't fathom what had possessed Uncle Drosselmeyer into giving her one as a present. Maybe Mama was right. Maybe in his old age he was going a little loopy after all.

Nevertheless, Clara didn't want to hurt his feelings. "Thank you Uncle." she said with a warm smile.

"Don't be foolish, girl." he said, cranky all of a sudden. "I know you don't like it. But this one is special to me. You must promise to keep it safe, no matter what happens."

"I will." she assured him. It was probably something from the olden days of Germany, then, if it meant that much to him. Maybe her uncle was trying to cling onto his past just as desperately as she was clinging onto hers. She had no right to judge.

Clearly satisfied with whatever it was Clara had said, Uncle Drosselmeyer sank back into the chair, a sly smile on his lips. "Good. Good.

Thank you Clara. You have done me a great favour. I can be at peace now."

And with that he picked up his cane and pushed himself to his wobbling feet before hobbling towards the door.

"Go steady, Uncle." Clara warned him.

"Do not fear for me, sweet niece. I will be fine. Everything is going to go entirely as planned." He smiled at her, his yellowing teeth showing, and left.

As he disappeared down the corridor, Clara let out a sigh she didn't realise she had been holding. He'd never behaved like that before, and it was almost eerie. She'd have a word with Mama about him in the coming days.

Realising she was still on the floor, she got up and sat down in the now-empty Chesterfield. The whisky she'd consumed earlier was beginning to get to her, and she felt warm and sleepy. The sounds of the party reverberated down the corridor, but Clara had no interest in rejoining it. She was so very tired, and the Chesterfield was so very comfy. No one would miss her if she spent a few minutes resting.

She snuggled down and immediately fell fast asleep, the nutcracker still in her hand.

CHAPTER FIVE
A CHRISTMAS CURSE

The clocks were striking twelve.

Clara awoke with a jolt. How could it possibly be midnight already? She had only meant to close her eyes for a moment or two! Ferdy and Mama were going to be so disappointed in her when they found out she'd slept through the whole of the evening.

And then she realised something: the entire house was silent.

She pushed herself up from where her head had been slumped on the chair arm and looked about. Not only was the house silent, it was in darkness. There was no light emitting from the hallway, and there was no chatter or Christmas carols to be heard. The party must have finished.

In the back of her mind, however, Clara sensed that the atmosphere was not just one of a finished party – for what high society party finished at midnight anyway? – but one of something much more sinister. For now she saw that the shadow was not of the blackness of night but lit by something more akin to moonlight, colouring everything in the inky, deep blue hue of Arctic ocean waters – and, now she thought about it, it was just as cold. Clara hugged her arms over her bare shoulders and shivered.

Something was very, very wrong.

She stood up out of the Chesterfield, and as she did, something clattered to the ground. Looking down, she saw her uncle's nutcracker grinning up at her. Slowly, she bent and retrieved it. Holding the figure to her chest, she quietly stepped out of the door and into the hallway.

Clara's breath fogged in front of her as she crept down the corridor. Nobody was there. They had all gone. Yet, as she continued on, she realised now that she could indeed hear something; not the sound of music or voices, but a sound that made the hair on the back of her neck stand up, a sound that should have had no place in a house at all. It changed in frequency; one moment it sounded like the sad, lonely calls whales used to speak to one another; another moment it sounded like the wind howling in a gale; and in another moment a metallic twang would reverberate loudly around the empty house, causing Clara to jump. Her eyes grew wide and terrified. She knew that noise. It was the creaks and moans of deeply-frozen ice as it cracked and shifted, entrapping whatever was in it in terrible permafrost and creating an impenetrable fortress that could only be liberated by the spring's warm sun.

Suddenly, for the first time since she had woken, Clara had a clear, sensible thought. She had to be dreaming! Maybe she had been dreaming ever since she had seen the mouse in the red waistcoat – all that had happened since had certainly been strange enough to warrant it. Wanting to test her theory, she tried the well-known trick that would determine the truth: she pinched herself.

It hurt.

She wasn't dreaming. This was real.

Something snapped inside Clara then, and she screamed; a loud, shrill, horrified scream. It made her throat hoarse and her eyes squeeze shut, but Clara couldn't help it. She screamed and screamed and screamed in terror, compacting all her fear into one appalling note. The nutcracker was still smiling in her hand as if he thought this was funny, and abruptly she could stand the horrid thing no longer and threw it the full length of the corridor. It bounced and landed several feet away.

Clara gulped as the rawness of her shout subsided. She was shaken and scared witless, but she doubted that standing in the hallway shrieking was going to do much to improve her circumstances. Fraught with indecision, she pushed back her hair from her face, wiped her eyes on the back of her hand and went to pick up the nutcracker. She hated it, but a promise was a promise, so she'd better take the damn thing with her.

She ran then, right back to the grand staircase. The noises of the ice sounded louder now, and it unnerved her. The great grandfather clock loomed against the wall like an alert soldier, its hands stuck firmly at midnight.

"Ferdy! Mama! Pyotr!" She tried calling out to her family. If they were anywhere in the house, they'd definitely be able to hear her from the hall.

Nothing.

Clara's breath caught as she started hyperventilating. She was shuddering now, and almost on her knees with cold. Then another idea came to her and she went towards the front door. Twisting the handle, she pulled it back – only to be met by a wall of fresh white snow, the outer markings of the door having been imprinted onto its powdery mass.

Clara stepped back, stumbling over her own feet, and ran towards the kitchen. She pulled open the back door, only to be met by a similar wintry blockade.

There was no way out. She was trapped.

Clara shook her head. This made absolutely no sense. Where were her loved ones? Why had the party guests vanished? Why was her house, her beloved Sweetmeadow Place, inexplicably entombed in snow and ice as if it had never once borne witness to the sun?

There had to be an escape, somehow.

Sprinting back to the grand hallway, she took the stairs two at a time, and then when she reached the stairwell for The Nook, she took the steps there as fast as she dared as well, climbing up and up, hoping to get some sort of answers, hoping she could at last see, now, what was wrong –

Her foot slipped on the last step, and she fell forwards.

With a yelp, Clara threw out her hand and wrapped it around the banister in order to break her fall, but her grip did not hold. Struggling to gain purchase on the steps she had climbed since she was a child, Clara looked down and saw that they too were completely covered in thick, slick ice. Not only that, but the banister was too, and it was dripping, emitting an echo as it did so.

Clara let out a little noise of defeat. She was tired, confused and scared. What was going on?

She gritted her teeth. She would figure it all out later. Right now, she just had to get to The Nook.

Ignoring the cold that bit into her aching fingers, she took tight hold of the banister, and with a fierce cry of determination, flung herself upwards, leaping over the last step and landing hard and awkwardly on her bedroom floor.

Gasping, Clara got to her feet. Her chin felt a little bruised, but it wasn't bleeding. She grabbed the nutcracker from where he had fallen at the side of her and staggered over to her bed, putting the figurine down on the covers. Then she hastily opened her suitcase and rifled through her things. Getting changed in this environment and temperature was certainly something to be braved, but she had no choice; any longer in this silly, flimsy little dress and she really would be hypothermic.

She tried not to flinch as she let the dress fall, snatching the brown boots, black thermal leggings, thick blue jumper and white, fur-lined coat she had found and tugging them all on quickly. When at last she was fully clothed, she was still cold, but she was no longer freezing. She picked up the nutcracker and slid him into the large interior pocket of her coat.

That dealt with, she went over to her desk, where she had put her phone for safekeeping whilst she had been at the party. Her fingers were rapidly numbing, but she still managed to find the power button and pressed it down. Like a beacon of hope, the screen lit up – only to tell Clara that she had no service. Beyond frustrated, and starting to feel just a little bit hopeless, she threw the phone down on the bed in disgust.

Knowing that she was running out of options, but still not understanding what exactly had led her to this point, she went and looked out of the window. Snow was falling heavily outside, adding to the mammoth drift that had barricaded the back door like a small mountain. In fact, now she looked at it, the pile was almost covering the entire first storey of the rear of the house. Maybe if she broke the window, Clara could jump out onto it. It wouldn't necessarily mean that she was free of this nightmare, but at least she'd be free of this ghost house that had no one in it and was smothered by ice.

She looked around her room for something heavy to knock the glass out with. As the seat prevented the window from going all the way down to the floor, she couldn't just push her desk through it. It needed to be something she could lift. But this was her bedroom, and it was filled to the brim with soft furnishings, which, whilst lovely most of the time, weren't useful in any way at all now.

Suddenly, she had it – the statue of the ballerina she kept on her bookshelf, the one

Mama had given her for Christmas when she was seven! It was weighty, and Mama had told her at the time that she must be careful with it, for if she dropped it would break beyond repair. Quickly, she ran over to the shelf and grabbed it.

And something squealed at her.

Clara squealed back, and suddenly both voices were yelling in surprise, their pitches getting higher and higher as they continued. Eventually, Clara calmed herself, and she peered on the shelf at whatever it was that had surprised her.

It was the little brown waistcoat-wearing mouse.

"You!" they cried simultaneously.

Clara gasped. "You can talk?"

"Of course I can." said the mouse rather crossly. He looked highly vexed at having been disturbed.

"Well, it wouldn't be the strangest thing that's happened all day." Clara muttered under her breath.

"Pardon?"

"Nothing."

"I think you're being rather rude. Humans are always rude. For instance, I was just about to go down to the dining room to get myself some dinner – there was an incredible banquet on tonight, let me tell you – and then some reckless individual invoked the Clock-Stop Curse and now it's all gone and I'm hungry and cold to the point where my tail may as well just be an icicle because this jacket does absolutely nothing to prevent frostbite! Do you know what day it is? It's Christmas Eve! No creature should be stirring, not even me!"

"I'm sorry about that, but... what did you say about a curse?"

The mouse sighed irritably. "The Clock-Stop Curse. It makes time stand still, if someone says the right words."

"You mean words like: 'into time's embrace I wish to delve, and make the clocks stop at the stroke of twelve'?"

"Yes, that would work – wait a minute. How do you know that?"

Clara gave him an apologetic look.

"You? You invoked the curse? Oh, fabulous! Wonderful!" he huffed. He marched away and jumped up on to a higher shelf.

"Look, I'm sorry! I didn't know what I was saying. It just kind of... slipped out. One minute I was talking to my uncle, then I fell asleep, and the next thing I know..." she gestured around vaguely. "I have no idea what to do now."

"Isn't it obvious?" The mouse scoffed from where he looked down at her from his lofty vantage point. "You have to go into The Land of Light, meet your heart's truest delight, and make the clocks all good and right."

"The what?"

"The Land of Light! You know, where the birds all sing for you, time has no end and dreams come true? No? Huh..."

"Look, little mouse —"

"My name is Bertram von Cheesesniffle, thank you, not 'little mouse'. Or should I just call you 'reckless human'?"

"Fair point. My name is Clara."

"Hm. Not bad, but I prefer 'reckless human' more." He scampered back down the bookcase and went to go and sit on the floor at Clara's feet.

"You seem to know a lot about this Land of Light, Bertram." Clara mused. "Do you think you could help me find it, if that's what I need to do to get out of here?"

"I knew that was coming." Bertram grumbled. "I warn you, my services have a fee."

"Which is?"

"Safe passage inside one navy jumper until we get to wherever it is we're going."

"Done." agreed Clara, and she held out her sweater sleeve, which Bertram scurried up. A few moments later, after much tickling and wriggling, he reappeared, poking his head out of her collar.

"Okay. First things first: we've got to find a way of getting out of here."

"I tried. The doors are covered with snowdrifts."

"Well then you didn't try very hard, did you? Come on, let's go." He slipped down back inside, peeping out through the knitted wool.

Being mindful of the slippery stairs, Clara descended and took herself and Bertram across the grand hallway.

"I don't know what change you expect there to be." Clara told him as she went to open the door. "Look."

Bertram cocked his head on one side as he regarded the snow. "Ah yes. That's quite a conundrum. But it will melt."

"Not any time soon." Clara declared miserably.

"Well, we're not going to get anywhere with an attitude like that, are we? Have you tried... oh, I don't know... believing it will melt?"

"What good will that do?"

"All I'm saying is that a little belief and imagination goes a long way."

Clara huffed. "The snow is going to melt." she said half-heartedly.

Nothing budged.

"Maybe with a bit more gusto." whispered Bertram.

Clara closed her eyes. "The snow is going to melt." she said again, more determined this time. Despite herself, in her mind's eye she could see a weak yet warm sun, heating the great mound and making it dissolve and fade to nothing but water. When she once more her voice was more resolute. "The snow is going to melt. The snow is going to melt!"

Clara was stunned to silence as she opened her eyes and saw the snow begin to move and shift as if she had cast an enchantment on it. It crumpled in on itself, collapsed and then blew away on a strong wind, as if it had never been there. Where there had once been an obstacle, now there was nothing. She was free to go as she pleased.

"See! What did I tell you?" cried Bertram cockily.

"But I don't understand..." Clara thought aloud.

"It's Christmas Eve. Anything could happen."

And with one last quick glance around Sweetmeadow Place, Clara Stahlbaum and Bertram von Cheesesniffle went out into the night.

CHAPTER SIX
FATHER WINTER

The wind whipped the snow into icy
needles so that it fell, as abrasive as sand, onto
Clara's exposed cheeks. She couldn't say how
long she and Bertram had been walking for, but
it felt like a very long time. Now, Clara just
stood, sore and aching, as her feet throbbed in
the dunes of flakes and the blizzard blew so fast
past her face that it obscured her vision; not that
she could have seen anything anyway, due to the
thick clouds that shielded everything beyond a

few feet of her from view, sucking the entire world into darkness.

It was a directionless maze of white, grey and blue, and she was lost inside it.

"You told me you could take me to The Land of Light!" she yelled at Bertram over the sounds of the weather.

"I said no such thing!" he yelled back. "You just assumed!" He was trying to sound confident, but in reality his whiskers were twitching rather nervously.

Clara squinted, but she could see nothing; no landmarks, roads or anything that would have given her some bearing as to where she found herself. She was disconsolate and disorientated, and the entire events of the night were rapidly proving to be too much for her. The wind buffeted her, and she reminded herself of the tiny glitter globe with The Eiffel Tower in it that her Mama had brought her back from a friend's hen do in Paris, the one that sat on the desk in The Nook at home.

A home she might never see again.

At this thought, her anger and frustration towards this supposed adventure mounted. "This is ludicrous!" she growled. The anger rose and rose inside her, until she threw back her head and shouted at the sky: "Father, make it stop!"

Immediately, the snowflakes halted in mid-air, the flurries dissipating, and the wind died down. The clouds did not give way, nor did moonlight appear, but that did not matter. The storm, which had assaulted Clara and Bertram since the moment they had left home, had come to an abrupt standstill.

"Is your father by any chance a wizard?" Bertram asked.

"No."

Suddenly, the heavy, dull silence was broken by a deafening, fearsome roar.

"Erm, Clara... what was that?" Bertram queried, his ears sticking up like satellite dishes.

The roar sounded again, a little louder this time.

"I think now might be a good time to run." Bertram suggested.

Before they could however, thudding deep footsteps could be heard, along with panting breaths. Whatever was coming in the snow, it was coming fast, advancing with a lumbering stride, and it sounded big.

Finally, the mist parted, and it revealed a monstrous polar bear, which bore down on Clara with a snarling bellow. His white fur glistened with frost as steam blew from his snout, his open mouth showing a row of sharp polished teeth. Muscles rippled in his shoulders and belly, and Clara just knew, instinctively, that the extended claws that curved out like carving knives from his great paws could fell her and tear her to ribbons in just one swift swipe, if he was so inclined.

She was paralysed with fear. Even as the polar bear sniffed at her she found she could not move, and stayed rooted to the spot. She simply held her ground and prayed that she would not startle him in any way that would provoke him to attack.

The bear growled again, and this time Clara shrank back, though she could not tear her eyes away from its mighty jaws. Deep down from somewhere inside her jumper, she felt Bertram quivering.

"Woah! Easy boy, easy!"

Clara jerked her head up. There, sat astride the massive bear, was a man. Or at least, Clara thought it was a man; it was hard to tell underneath all the layers. He wore heavy dark blue robes of warming velvet that cascaded over his mount's flanks, and they looked old and travel-worn, as if they had fallen victim to some hungry moths over the years. A leather belt around his waist held small vials that contained mysterious shimmering liquids in them, and an amulet of brilliant blue crystal cut into a teardrop shape hung around his neck. His hair was platinum white, and was so long it was impossible to tell where his hair stopped and his beard, which fell like a stalactite to his naval, began. Wise blue eyes shone like jewels in the creases and crevasses of his eons-old face.

Despite his appearance however, when his spoke his voice was as welcoming as mulled wine in midwinter. "Goodness me, child! Whatever happened that you should be out here in weather such as this, so far away from home? It's no place for a lass like you. No wonder you called on me to stop it!"

"W-well, a-a-actually, I didn't. I mean, not on purpose." Clara stammered. She was still acutely aware of the bear's nostrils hovering in close proximity to her face.

The old man chuckled. "Perhaps it's a good job you did." He swung down off the bear and landed in the snow next to Clara, snow crunching under his faded brown leather boots as he did so. "Sometimes I can get a little carried away."

He trudged around to the front of the bear and dug in his pocket, retrieving a lump of red, fatty meat and holding it in front of the beast's face. He cooed at the animal as if it was nothing but an obedient puppy, and then, just as gently, the bear took the flesh from his fingers.

"Seal." the old man explained when he saw Clara looking. "His favourite."

The bear, having finished his mouthful, licked his lips and nodded slightly, as if he was approving.

"He's friendly?"

"Of course! Why, there's no need to be scared of old Eisvang here. He's as gentle as they come!" He stroked the bear's hefty head to show that he was tame. In response, the immense creature growled softly and gave the man a playful head butt.

"So if he's Eisvang, who are you?" asked Clara innocently.

The man turned and raised a bushy eyebrow at the girl, but he said nothing.

"Way to go, Clara!" Bertram hissed. "You've just insulted one of the greatest magical spirits of all time!"

"But who is he?" Clara whispered. Maybe the mouse could tell her and spare her from further embarrassment.

"He's —"

"I am Father Winter." the man boomed in a deep voice that seemed too big given his slight, frail stature. "The Bringer of the Winds, The Shepherd in the Storm. And you, it seems, are lost."

"I'm trying to find my way to The Land of Light." the desperate girl informed him.

For a moment, Father Winter went as still as ice on a pond. Clara wondered if she had somehow offended him further.

Then he started laughing.

"The Land of Light, you say! Well you won't find it out here, that's for sure!" He wiped away the tears that his chortling had caused. Then he saw Clara's face. "Sorry, I shouldn't laugh. Perhaps you could come to my home, for some hospitality? I can explain everything to you while you warm up." He smiled kindly at her.

"Thank you."

With a sly smile, Father Winter clambered back onto Eisvang. Then, leaning over, he stretched out his hand to her.

"Come on." he said, as merriment twinkled in his eyes.

"Ride on a polar bear?" Bertram squeaked. "You can't be serious!"

But Clara wasn't sure that this was a night for being serious. She put her hand in Father Winter's and he hauled her, behind him, onto Eisvang. To his credit, the bear didn't move or show discomfort, not even as Clara settled into her straddle aboard the bear's back and gently took his fur in her hands for support.

"What I wouldn't give to be at home with some cheese right now." sighed Bertram from his seat on Clara's shoulder.

Then, with another ear-shattering call, Eisvang took off at full charge into the wasteland, and the snow began to fall again.

CHAPTER SEVEN
ICE MAGIC

For how long they rode Clara could not say. It
could have been days, hours or minutes. Not
that it mattered any more. Not now that she had
cursed the clocks to stop and time was an
abstract concept. She simply closed her eyes and
stuffed her hands up her sleeves as Bertram
curled around her fingers in an effort to keep
himself warm, and Eisvang's forceful bulk
charged onwards towards a non-changing,
invisible horizon.

Eventually though, Clara felt the land begin to slope, as if they were going downhill. As she wakened from her chill-induced stupor and opened her eyes, she saw that the polar bear was descending a hillock with a surprisingly delicate tread. The place was ensconced in solitude, and tall hills encompassed either side of the valley, wrapping everything in a stony embrace as they reached towards the sky.

For all the time that she had spent exploring this area in her youth, Clara had never been here before. True, the clocks had stopped, but they couldn't have travelled so far that the landscape could have changed so dramatically, could they?

Turning away from the hills she looked over Eisvang's ears, and when she saw what he was heading towards her eyes grew wide. For there, at the foot of the dense white knoll, shielded from the worst of the weather by a copse of pine trees, was a homely log cabin, with smoke belting from its chimney and lights glowing invitingly at the leaded windows. Instead of being small however, it was large, with a high vaulted roof that made it look almost like a barn, and the double front doors, which she assumed were made from oak, were carved with the images of mountains.

"My home." explained Father Winter, looking back at Clara with a straight posture and just a hint of pride.

"It's lovely." Clara said, and she meant it. Despite being surrounded by the wrath of the winter, the house, which now grew ever-closer, seemed a snug and sturdy oasis.

As they reached the foot of the hill and a trench that had been dug to give access, Eisvang snorted softly and came to an abrupt stop. Clara, Bertram and Father Winter slid off the animal, the snow cushioning their landing, and trudged up to the front door. To Clara's surprise, Eisvang followed them.

Father Winter spread his two broad hands on the entrance and pushed slightly. With a creak they opened right to the apex of the roof, creating a space big enough for Eisvang to comfortably go through. Clara and Bertram went in first, and then the great bear, and when they were all inside Father Winter shut the door behind him and then ran over to the grate to fuss and stoke the fire.

As the embers brought the house to life, Clara found herself in a dwelling that was little more than a glorified trapper's hut. The walls and floor were wooden and undecorated, and the amenities were few; there was only a small stove, and an even smaller dining table. Dried fish hung from the beams, along with various other meats, prepared for smoking, that Clara had no wish to identify. Eisvang ate seal; it had to be stored somewhere.

Nevertheless it was a warm and welcoming shelter from the weather; heaving shelves stored bric-a-brac, an old wooden staircase led to a cosy loft space that made a bedroom, and there were comfortable chairs seated around the fire. Clara deposited herself in one as the flames took hold.

Before Clara could open her mouth to start asking questions, she was interrupted by someone very small tiptoeing down her sleeve and out onto the chair arm.

"Excuse me, Father Winter sir, but I am a very cold and hungry mouse, and I don't suppose... you have any cheese?"

"Bertram!" Clara scolded softly, but Father Winter laughed cheerfully.

"Where are my manners? Of course —
Bertram, is it? Yes. Yes Bertram, of course you
can have some cheese."

Father Winter went to the kitchen and
came back with a whole stack of the finest
cheddar, which he put in front of the mouse.

"Now this is living!" Bertram cried, and
dove headfirst into the pile, his tail being the
only part of him that remained visible.

Father Winter chuckled. "And something
for you, my dear. That'll warm your cockles." he
said as he passed Clara a cup of something hot,
steaming and red in colour. Tentatively, she took
a sip. The liquid instantly warmed her up from
the inside, and it tasted deliciously of red berries
and cinnamon. She liked it very much.

Once he had seen that all his guests were comfortable, Father Winter sat himself down in the chair across from Clara. Eisvang plodded into the space between them, and with a thud he laid in front of the hearth like a living throw rug, close to Father Winter's feet.

"Now then, lass. Tell me, how exactly did you come to be standing in the middle of a winter storm, and one brought on by The Clock-Stop Curse at that? That's no place for a slip of a thing like you. Please, tell me all that you know. That way I can advise you on how best to continue." Father Winter said gravely.

Quickly, Clara brought him up to speed.

When he had finished listening to her story, his hand resting contemplatively on his chin, he sat forward and spoke. "I see. Well, at least the curse was of your own invoking. That makes things a bit easier. Terrible business, to be caught up in someone else's magic."

"This is magic?

"Aye."

So how do we get to The Land of Light?" Clara demanded. She was starting to get frustrated with everyone speaking in riddles.

"Ah, child, impatience is a trait so common in your kind. It baffles me beyond all else." he said, bemused.

"There are things, Clara, which the human race – your race – cannot comprehend. Not because they are stupid, nay, but because many things are hidden from them. There is not just your world, but a great many, bound next to each other like pages in a book. They can be reached, if a person knows how. No matter what plane of existence you inhabit, however, there is only one goal: to reach The Land of Light. In your world, your Plane, The Land of Light is called Heaven, or something similar, and it is known by many other names across many other Planes too. It itself is a Plane consisting of all the good things you can think of: happiness and love, yes, but also imagination and belief."

"Wait a second..." Clara suddenly had a startling thought. "Am I... is this a different Plane to the one I'm from?"

"Smart girl. Yes, you are currently in The Hinterworld; on your Plane, it is often known as Limbo."

"But I'm not... I can't be..."

"Oh goodness no! You're not dead! But you did speak a curse that stopped time, which enabled you to slip between Planes."

"I don't even know how I did that. Besides, how can that theory even be possible? It can't be! I saw Bertram on my Plane, wearing his waistcoat –"

"And you thought you were mad. Yes. Glitches in the Planes, thanks to temporary overlaps, tend to result in that reaction."

Clara looked at her feet, dumbfounded. Father Winter leaned forward.

"I know this is a delicate question my child, but I have to ask. One does not stop the clocks without meaning to, without intent. There must have been a reason you felt that you needed to halt time in order to find a way to The Land of Light, for it will contain your heart's delight."

Stunned, Clara felt in the lining of her coat for the nutcracker she had been carrying and took it out. She had no idea why, but it felt pivotal to her explanation.

"I wanted to go back to what it was like before." she whispered quietly, looking down at the wooden figure. "I wanted to see my father again. He died. I miss him."

At this, Father Winter nodded solemnly. For all his infinite wisdom, he knew there was nothing he could say that would assuage the girl's deep grief. "Then that must be what awaits you in The Land of Light. That is how all this will stop and begin again. You froze time so that you were free to seek out your wish and make your dream come true."

"I can't see my father again!" Clara cried. "That's impossible!"

"Only if you choose to believe it is impossible."

"Clara..." piped up Bertram from his heap of cheese, where he had momentarily stopped stuffing his greedy little face. "The Land of Light is a Plane consisting of everything you could ever think of. It has no laws. If your father is what you wished for, I'll have no doubt he'll be there, waiting for you."

The young woman was quiet for a minute before continuing, and when she did she addressed Father Winter. "Journeying to The Land of Light is the only way I can get home, right? Regardless of whether my father is there or not. So why is no one telling me how to get there?"

"Would you know the pathway to Heaven?" Father Winter queried, a slight smile on his lips. "Look inside yourself, Clara. This is your path to take."

Clara almost rolled her eyes; it was so cryptic and so stereotypical of every 'chosen one' movie she'd ever seen. If what she had remembered of those silly stories was correct, she had to go into a trance or something equally tedious, while they all stared at her and her eyes popped open and she whispered a name in some long-forgotten language, which either Bertram or Father Winter would then later attempt to translate. It was all so preposterous.

But then again, she was trapped in an unending icy purgatory with a talking mouse and The Shepherd in the Storm, so she had to try. She closed her eyes, settled back in her warm chair and waited for something mystical to happen. A few moments passed. Nothing occurred. She felt a burning embarrassment at having to do such a thing. Her father would never —

Her father.

All at once a blinding flash exploded behind her eyelids and she saw him, her Papa, his face filled with all the kindness and joy she remembered him to have, illuminated by rays of something so pure it brought tears to her eyes. He reached towards her with an outstretched hand, and in her mind Clara took it, walking with him as he came to a building that was built from blocks of ice so clear it was almost like glass, that was so tall its tops could not be seen as it rose up into the oppressive clouds of The Hinterworld. The building stood as silent as a tomb, unmovable and primordial as the landscape. The dense ice door that graced its face swung back on its thick rivets with a shudder, almost as if it was being pulled back by the hand of a phantom. And then, without warning, her father stepped into it.

Clara wanted to scream at him to stay with her, to beg him to stop. She opened her mouth, but no sound emitted except a strange metallic echo. In one last desperate act, she lunged for her Papa – and was immediately propelled back in front of the fire at the home of Father Winter.

"You did it Clara!" cried Bertram jubilantly. "Just like at your house with the snow!"

But Clara wasn't listening. "There's a fort!" Clara gasped as her companions looked at her with concern. "A fort made of ice, on the ice. The path to The Land of Light... I can find it there!"

Father Winter nodded. "Yes. That sounds like The Fortress of Forgotten Things."

From out of the corner of her eye, Clara swore she could have seen Bertram flinch, but she wasn't sure why. Taking his reaction as a cue, she asked: "How do we get there then?"

"It is not the destination that is the problem. You must be careful, Clara. The Hinterworld can be a dangerous place, fraught with dangerous things."

"Like what?" she challenged.

"We are ruled here by a tyrant. He is called The Mouse King, and he's as weasel-like and wicked as any rodent could ever be. We never see him, for he sits high in his keep, called Mausburg, and dispatches his legions to do his bidding. You must have your wits about you if you are to survive this. It's why I have to live on the edge like this now. I have been pursued, and he would try and take everything I have from me given the chance."

Clara looked the snow king confidently in the eye. "All the fear left in me vanished the day my Papa passed."

Father Winter held her gaze for a moment and then he strode past her, unhooking some of the smoked meats from the beams above her head and passing them to her. She tucked them in her coat pocket beside the nutcracker and thanked him as he presented her with a pair of warm, thick gloves that looked as if they were made from reindeer hide or something similar, along with a pair of matching, flat boots that had neat stitching along the soles and uppers and were lined with fur.

"You will have a long way to travel, and whilst the weather is at my command, I cannot protect you from the adverse effects of its coldness. I regret that, but this is the way it has to be. This is the path you have chosen. Therefore, I give you these, for they are so warm that your hands and feet will never feel a chill no matter how far you go."

"Father, you are too kind." Clara said as she pulled off her own footwear and slid into his magical ones. Almost immediately the throbbing aches in her toes subsided and were replaced by a rather pleasant radiating warmth that seemed to ward off any draught that had a mind to seek her out. She tugged on the gloves, and her fingers did the same. She smiled at him. "Thank you for your gifts and hospitality Father, but I think we'd better be going now, especially if we don't want to catch the attention of The Mouse King."

"Wait, please. That is not all. I have no desire to send you out on this journey alone. I cannot come with you, sadly, for I must bring the winds, but you will need help, should you ever wish to return to the human Plane."

The ancient wizard walked away from her and put his hands on the window. Almost immediately, hoarfrost began to form at his fingertips and creep across the frame; hoarfrost that solidified in mass and weight until it was seeping in through the glass. Despite the warm temperature of the room however, it did not melt but froze where it was cast, fractals forming spindly, jagged spikes as it curved and spun, creating a shape above the floorboards.

Clara squinted at it. She wasn't sure if her eyes were deceiving her, but there was something about the freezing wave that made it appear almost human.

She looked towards Father Winter and saw that he had his eyes closed, as if he was concentrating intensely. Intrigued, Clara's head swivelled back in the direction of his magic, and now she could see it; the ice was no longer a wave but was developing into the shape of someone slight and elfin, someone most undeniably blue in skin tone. Pointed toes were attached to slender ankles, which were attached to stick-thin legs. The torso was narrow, almost skeletal, the neck thin, and the face had sharp angled jawbones that highlighted two very large eyes, a defined nose and a wide mouth. Atop the head was a shock of crystalline hair that would have looked to be one with the skin were it not for the pale glimmers that refracted through the spiky shards. Clara couldn't help but wince; the being, who was about as tall as Clara herself, was so fragile she feared it would break in half if it so much as moved one inch forward.

The being now completed, the excess ice simply faded away into nothing, leaving only the delicate little creature standing lightly on his tiptoes, as if he were preparing to perform a jig of some kind. He really was the most brilliant hue Clara had ever seen, like the colour of water droplets that ran off a kingfisher's back. His eyes were still closed, and he appeared to be sleeping.

Father Winter walked up to him and placed his hands on his creation's shoulders, and Clara saw a small amount of steam escape the man, as if he were defrosting a little. After a few moments the creature stirred and awoke, revealing the most disturbingly beautiful ghostly grey irises with no pupils, so that he appeared to have no vision at all. In fact, Clara would have believed that to be the case, had he not grinned widely when his gaze had turned on her, revealing, sharp, needle-like teeth.

"This is Shiverfinger." Father Winter said by way of introduction. "He will be your guide and take you to The Fortress of Forgotten Things."

Neither Clara nor Shiverfinger said anything in response to this. After a few moments of stony silence however, the ice sprite rolled his head on his neck and arched his shoulders.

And that was when Clara saw them.

She could only watch as a set of wings unfurled themselves from the middle of Shiverfinger's back, trailing behind him like an opalescent train. They were dragonfly-like in their shape, narrower nearer the base and rounder towards the tip, with deep blue veins running through them like a spider web sparkled with dew. Each one was about double the height of Shiverfinger himself, and they stood protruding at a diagonal angle from his shoulder blades.

He caught Clara's gaze again, and then, without warning, took to the air and flew forwards a few meters, his wings emitting a vibrating thrum as he did. As soft as thistledown, he alighted in front of the girl, looking at her fixedly, his blind eyes looking directly into her own and then flickering about, as if he were somehow searching her soul for an answer he could not quite find. Gently, he took one of Clara's ringlets and absentmindedly weaved it through his spindle-like fingers.

"Pretty fairy." he mused, his whispery voice sounding like a squall that would bring foreboding conditions.

"Oh, I'm not a fairy." Clara replied, equally quietly. She found herself enraptured by the sprite, rather than terrified; there was so much grace and surety within him that he was quite ethereal.

Shiverfinger shook his head. "No. You pretty fairy. I say."

Clara smiled. His strange, broken way of talking was oddly endearing, like a child that had grasped only the basics of speech. She knew, however, that he wasn't dumb; whatever he was seeing behind those visionless orbs was simply more than he could accurately voice. Realising that using too many words might simply overwhelm him, she tried to copy instead. "You take me and mouse to Fortress of Forgotten Things?"

Shiverfinger bowed deeply. "I know way and I protect you, pretty fairy. I promise."

She turned to look at Father Winter. "He's beautiful."

"I'm glad you like him. He will keep you safe whilst you travel on."

Shiverfinger looked between Clara and Father Winter and back again. "We go now?"

When Clara spoke her tone was decisive and final. "Yes, Shiverfinger. We go now."

CHAPTER EIGHT
AVALANCHE

Now that she had Father Winter's enchanted boots and gloves upon her feet and hands, the cold did not seem to bother Clara as much anymore. The snow had given them a reprieve, and as such the clouds had cleared, giving way to a night in which Clara could see scatterings of beautiful stars as they shone, and the moon, which was full and coated the landscape with a luminous, ghostly glow. Shiverfinger swooped in the air above Clara, seemingly doing aerial acrobatics just for the sheer fun of it as he called down directions to her. Walking along on such a magical night with friends, when the stars were bright, made Clara's heart glad in a way that she had not felt in a long time. Now that the driving storm had abated, The Hinterworld was not as barren as she had once thought; the mountains were stark, yes, but there were trees to cover them some of the way, creating small inlets where the shadows danced and magical beings might just be hiding.

Only Bertram was skittish; he ran back and forth across Clara's shoulders, trying to get a better view of what was going on, and then retreated down the neck of her jumper once he got too cold.

"You're very impatient." Clara observed.

"The sooner we get to The Fortress of Forgotten Things the better." declared Bertram as he pulled his waistcoat further around his shoulders. "This is no place for any of us to be. And I would appreciate it if you told the ice sprite to keep it down. His hollering is making me nervous."

Shiverfinger heard them talking and swooped low over Clara's head whilst whooping loudly. "Mouse is afraid, afraid of what's to come! But I know way! Walk along this western crag, up past the highest peak, down the steepest slope below and across the fields bleak! See? Father Winter told me everything, and I know way!"

Clara giggled.

"Stop it!" said Bertram tersely. "We're on a mission, you know! Take it seriously!"

"What's got into you?" Clara demanded. "There's nothing to be afraid of out here; not even The Mouse King could find us! Look!"

She strode towards a small clearing that was covered in snow, and continued on through it. The gap led to a cliff edge that overlooked The Hinterworld, which shimmered under the spectral lunar light, pine trees casting dark silhouettes and the mountains huddling around it all. The tundra was simply a wonderland.

"See? It's beautiful."

"That's just the problem. I don't trust its beauty." Bertram sighed sadly.

Clara frowned at him. "Bertram? What do you fear?"

The mouse clambered off of her and shot over to a nearby rock, standing on his hind legs so that he could look her in the face. His feet shuffled nervously. "Clara, there's something I need to tell you. I'm... I'm not a brave mouse."

Clara smiled at him sympathetically, relieved he didn't have anything worse to say. "That's not true, Bertram. You're the bravest mouse I've ever met."

"That's not what I mean!" The little fellow seemed panicky now; he began pacing and pulling at his ears, and then he turned to his friend again and looked at her with big, imploring eyes. "Clara, I–"

The girl didn't have time to hear him. For just as Bertram was about to reveal whatever it was he was going to divulge, the ground beneath Clara shuddered as if it were unexpectedly partaking in an avalanche, and then suddenly gave way underneath her. Losing her footing, Clara screamed as she fell down the slippery ravine, and with a groan and all the strength she could muster she grabbed onto the ledge with both hands and willed her fingers to hold on.

Bertram shouted her name, but Clara did not call back. Instead, she risked a look down. The drop underneath her was far away; not enough to kill her, but she would probably sustain a few injuries if she fell. Holding on with all that she had, she heard Bertram calling again, this time for Shiverfinger, and she prayed that the ice sprite was nearby and would be able to lift her out of her current predicament; he might be thin, but his wings were powerful and could surely support both of their weight.

Abruptly, however, there was a commotion and whatever hope Clara might have had was destroyed as a piercing howl broke the sky. She looked up, above the cliff edge, and to her horror she saw ropes, seemingly coming out of nowhere, rise up towards Shiverfinger and pull him out of the sky, fastening around his wings and preventing him from getting anywhere near her, or even free. He crashed to the ground, bound by his tethers.

This wasn't an avalanche. They were under attack.

Before she could react, Clara heard a nearby cry and saw Bertram falling over the edge of the cliff, his small arms and legs flailing as he sped past her.

"No!" Clara cried. Instinctively, she pushed all her weight through one arm and strained to catch her friend. Then, with shock, she realised, as she dangled from the precipice like a precariously-tied bauble, that the nutcracker was falling out of her inner pocket. She saw it gradually teeter further and further, and then that spun away in a freefall too. Looking back up towards the edge, her expression became even more horrified as she saw that she was now clinging to the cliff by only the tips of her fingers. There was nothing more she could do; her grip failed her, gravity won and she plummeted.

She landed in the snow with a hard thud which winded her and knocked her senseless. She lay there for a while, stunned – and then she came to and scrambled to her feet, picking up the nutcracker as she ran.

"Bertram!" she cried as she hurried over to her lifeless companion. He was on his back, his legs in the air and his eyes closed, his waistcoat crumpled and torn slightly at one edge.

From somewhere further back up the cliff, Shiverfinger yelled again. Clara swallowed hard, bit down on her fear and hoped that he would be able to hold his own against their attackers. Right now, Bertram desperately needed her help; the bold, witty mouse was unresponsive and cold. Clara scooped him up and cradled him in the crook of her arm as if he were a broken baby doll.

"Bertram, Bertram! Come back to me! Please!"

Still he did not move.

"Bertram... I'm so sorry. You were right, we should have been more careful. I should have been more careful. I'm so sorry." She started to weep over his minuscule, inert body.

"Step away from the traitor!"

Clara shot upright in alarm. The voice that had spoken to her had been loud and authoritative, but there was no one to be seen; just the moon, the clouds and the never-ending snow.

"Down here, useless human!"

Clara looked where she was told, and then she gasped. For there, pointing miniature lances at her that looked very sharp even though they could have been no bigger than toothpicks... were an abundance of mice.

These mice, however, were nothing like Bertram; they did not have his warm brown fur or inquisitive eyes. Instead, their fur was the colour of rain-filled puddles, and their eyes were beady and filled with malice and mischief. They wore suits of battle-scarred armour that was dull given its amount of usage, and underneath, their livery was black edged with silver. The ringleader who had spoken stepped forward.

"I am Captain Tailtrod. By order of The Mouse King, you, the traitor and the ice sprite are now prisoners and are to come with us to Mausburg, and await His Majesty's justice."

"What are you going to do to me?" demanded Clara with courage in her voice. "You are nothing but mice! You can't hurt me!"

"Really? You've seen what we've done to your friends. What's to stop us from doing the same to you?" sneered Tailtrod.

Clara had no words to say in response; she was trapped, and she knew that the horrible Captain was right. She floundered helplessly. "You wouldn't dare!"

"Oh, but we would. Now, are you going to be a good girl and walk, or do we have to bind you too?"

"Fine. I'll come with you... on the condition that absolutely no harm comes to Bertram." She hugged her friend closely to her chest.

"Wouldn't dream of it." he told her. His comrades sniggered.

Then he signalled with his spear and his associates swarmed Clara and began to clamber all over her body.

"Stop, no!" she yelled.

The army didn't listen; instead they surged onwards until they reached her arms and,

overpowering the young woman, snatched
Bertram from her, dragging him away.

"No!"

The Captain laughed evilly. "You're far
too trusting, human girl." He turned to address
his troops. "Take them to the king."

And at his words the mass of mice, strong
in their numbers, pushed, shoved and pulled
Clara, Bertram and Shiverfinger into the
unknown, nipping them with their sharp, pointy
teeth as they went.

CHAPTER NINE
IN THE HALL OF THE MOUSE KING

When she had first entered The Hinterworld, Clara had been under the impression that it would go on forever. However, as it turned out, it did indeed come to an end; at a cave so dark and so foreboding that it looked as if some great beast had closed its yawning maw around the Plane. This was where the mouse legion stopped.

In front of her, some of their number carried Bertram aloft on their shoulders. Clara had watched him the entire time, but he had never once stirred. Behind her, Shiverfinger yowled, hissed and called out to her from his imprisonment inside the ropes.

There was nothing Clara could have done, for she herself was surrounded by mice; they milled around her feet, making sure that she kept moving forward and ensuring that she wasn't looking for an escape route. She knew, given her larger size, that she could have just stepped over the rodents... but she didn't want to think about what would happen to her friends as a consequence if she did.

"In." Captain Tailtrod directed her.

Clara hesitated for a moment, shrinking back from the entrance. She wanted to be brave, yet now she found herself consumed by terror at the notion of entering Mausburg. The opening was just about her height; she would have to duck, but that wasn't what was bothering her. It was the black, obsidian rocks that dripped with damp, stagnant water that made her cringe and shy away. To Clara, it really felt as if she were entering the mouth of Hell itself.

She stood there, fearful, and then she felt the Captain jab her in the heel with his staff, and she gave out a little indignant cry as he barked: "Get moving!"

All the mice-soldiers began to prick Clara's feet with their sharp staves, so that her feet lifted involuntarily as they twitched. Clara steeled herself. There was nowhere else to go but forward.

Under the ruthless command of the rodent army, she stepped into the gloom, and there was another great cry from Shiverfinger as they pulled him inside too. Immediately, she felt claustrophobic; the tunnels they had entered were impossibly dim, with jagged corners that stuck out and tore at Clara's legs. She stumbled blindly, cursing as she did and wondering why there was no light. Then she remembered: mice could see well in the dark. They wouldn't trouble themselves to illuminate their keep solely for the benefit of their prisoners.

They kept on and on and on, until it seemed to Clara that the mice were leading them right into the bowels of the earth. Shiverfinger, who was still protesting a ways behind Clara, did not go quietly, his shrieks and yells reverberating around the cavern.

"Shiverfinger, please." Clara tried reasoning with him. "Please don't shout. It'll be alright, I promise."

She twisted her torso so that she might look at her friend and give him a reassuring smile, but his ghostly eyes just stared back at her, shining with tears, his expression one of complete and utter sadness. It subdued Clara into silence.

"You should listen to your mistress, ice sprite!" Tailtrod spat meanly, and there was a whisper of titters from the other soldiers as he did so.

Clara said nothing against him. She had begun to accept that she was never going to make it to The Fortress of Forgotten Things, let alone The Land of Light. The clocks would be stopped forever, she would be stuck here forever, and the mice and their mysterious king would be able to do whatever they wanted with her forever.

Eventually though, they stopped marching. Clara was glad, for despite her magical boots and gloves from Father Winter, she was tired and knew she couldn't walk any more.

Then she saw what was in front of her, and she stopped feeling glad, because there, built into the heavy stone, was a cell, with giant, metal bars on the outwards-facing wall. Captain Tailtrod stepped forward and shimmied up one of these bars, then, from his gilet pocket, pulled out a small ring of intricate keys, and slipped one into the equally-small lock that was attached to the side of the cell. When the door, which was spring-loaded, swung open automatically, the mice pushed Clara and her friends inside.

Clara noted the door must have been on a timer, for after a few seconds the door swung shut again. She was powerless as Tailtrod locked them in and Shiverfinger began screeching once more.

"Please." said Clara as she rushed up to the bars, desperate to speak to the Captain before he disappeared. "We've done nothing wrong. I swear it."

"We'll see what the king thinks, shall we?" the mouse snarled at her before he dropped to the ground. He shouted an order at the rest of his legion, and they scurried away, down the network of tunnels.

Clara sank to the floor of the cell. It was so dark in here that she couldn't make out a single thing. Not even the moon could penetrate the cell. They were all alone; there were no other cells around them. She was cold and tired and hungry. Absentmindedly, she began pinching herself. If she couldn't get to The Land of Light, she would have to wake herself up by force.

Shiverfinger gave out a disconsolate moan. "Pretty fairy..."

At once, Clara hurried over and, by feel, undid his bonds, burning her hands on the ropes as she went. When he was finally free, Shiverfinger flexed his dishevelled wings, and then turned and looked at her with hurt eyes, close enough so that she could see them.

"Trick." he said simply.

Clara was nearly brought to tears by his innocence. "Yes, trick." she confirmed sadly.

Shiverfinger said nothing. Instead, as light as a feather, he rose up into the air, right to the ceiling of the cell. His feet dangled in Clara's face, but she did not care; she could only strain her eyes and watch, aggrieved, as the ice sprite started prising at the upper corners of the cell with his bare hands, his efforts becoming increasingly aggressive as he continued. Small stones bounced down around her as he groaned and grunted, but of course, the hardened rock wall did not give way.

"Shiverfinger, it's no use. Don't."

"But I know way! Father Winter say!"

"I know you do, but I don't think any of that matters anymore."

Shiverfinger's head drooped. He backed away from the walls and flew down to the floor, where he curled up in a ball, hugging his knees and making soft sobbing noises. Sinking down to his level, Clara peered at him and saw that he was crying, his tears solidifying into icicles as they tracked down his face. She used her thumb to wipe them away, trying not to flinch at the freezing water.

"We'll be alright." she assured him. "We'll stick together."

Again, Shiverfinger said nothing. Instead, he reached out and drew his friend into a warm – if slightly chilly – hug.

An immeasurable amount of time later, long after Clara's joints had stiffened and seized up, something moved at the side of her, something soft and almost imperceptible that groaned.

"Bertram!"

She flew away from Shiverfinger and groped for the mouse, cupping his head in the palm of her hand as she figured out the way he was laying. "Hey, hey. Take it easy. You fell."

Bertram nodded slightly. "I remember." Craning his neck, he tried to look around. "Where in the name of Edam are we?"

"Mausburg."

"Mausburg? Oh no. No. No! This cannot be happening!" He had turned pale with fear.

"Calm down, calm down! It'll be alright. We'll figure out an escape plan."

"No, trust me Clara, it will not be alright." He sat himself up, his head hanging morosely. "Remember when I told you I wasn't a brave mouse? This is what I was talking about."

A realisation slowly dawned on Clara. "You were one of them."

He looked up at her with grief in his eyes. "I'm a mouse. On this Plane, soldiers are what we are. But I tried not to be. I hid, for a long time. I was minding my own business one day, out there in the forest, when they found me and forced me to join their legions. But I couldn't stomach it. You think being captured was bad, the fake avalanche was bad? That's just the start of what they can do!"

"Which is?" quizzed Clara.

When Bertram looked up his eyes were haunted. "Everyone in The Hinterworld is afraid of them. Even Father Winter; when he said that the place was full of dangerous things, this is what he meant, remember. To many others, mice seem non-threatening, but in reality, they can eavesdrop in holes in the wall, slip poison into food unnoticed, start fires with the smallest bits of kindling... and they can chew. They'll chew anything that stands in their way."

Clara grimaced at the thought and held up a hand. "Okay. I really don't need to hear any more. What about this king though? What's he like?"

"Don't know. If you're not a high ranking mouse, you don't see him; he just sends orders, down from on high." Bertram put his head in his hands again. "We're just minions, to do his bidding. The others were too blind to see it, but I wasn't. Being a trained killer is no life for a mouse. I had to leave; I wanted a peaceful life again. I deserted my legion. Now, they'll execute me as a traitor."

"No. I won't let that happen."

Bertram let out a little non-humorous laugh. "Clara, your bravery and determination is admirable, but you'll be utterly defenceless against the king and his army."

Just at that moment, they heard a pair of scuttling feet advancing towards the cell.

"Well then, what do I do?" Clara asked him desperately.

He didn't have time to reply before Captain Tailtrod opened the door again, and when he spoke it was to Clara.

"His Majesty wants to speak with you." he informed her abruptly.

She knew better than to argue with him, and so, with a worried glance back at her friends, she went willingly. Bertram quietly mouthed 'good luck' at her as she left.

With Tailtrod walking ahead of her, Clara followed him through the arches and alleyways of the underground dungeons. From the nearby passageways, she could now hear the distressed voices of other prisoners calling out, yet she saw none of them.

After what seemed like a long while, however, the dungeon petered out and ended in a stairway, at the end of which was a heavy metal door. Tailtrod climbed upward and jumped on a lever that was next to it. As with the cell door, it sprung open automatically, and obediently Clara stepped through it. Up here, there was an unexpected great deal of light, and although she was temporarily blinded, eventually she could take in her new surroundings easily.

When she saw that she was standing in a grand, human-sized castle, her surprise was immeasurable.

The walls and floors were hewn from the stone of the great cave, and were decorated with tapestries and carpets of the grimmest colours. Some of the fabrics were embroidered, and when she looked at the stitching, she immediately wished she hadn't; she saw human enemies being swathed by mice, smaller enemies having their limbs torn off, and buildings and strongholds being overwrought with them. Bertram had been right. The mice of Mausburg used their seemingly innocent appearance to infiltrate and destroy any enemy without mercy. As she looked at the screaming, terrified faces immortalised in thread, she shuddered and made a promise to herself to keep her wits about her, like Father Winter had told her she'd need.

The castle was cold and an unforgiving wind danced about, the torches on the wall sputtering in their braziers. Clara could see through the windows that a newborn storm blew and fresh snow fell outside, and the noise that this made through the cracks in Mausburg's walls sounded like the cries of the dammed... or perhaps it was intermingling with them.

However, Clara was struck that the rodents should live in a human-sized building. Everything that she had seen so far, from the dungeon doors to the furniture she passed, had not been designed for mice at all. Once or twice she had had to watch her step to permit a passing sentry, or be careful to mind a guard standing to attention, somewhat ineffectively, by a comparatively giant doorframe. It seemed madness to her that rodents could live in a place like this, but then again, perhaps their egos were so inflated, they honestly thought that they were as big as the humans they had stolen this castle from. Clara wouldn't put it past them – and if the attitudes of the soldiers were anything to go by, then what was their monarch like?

After marching down a multitude of corridors, Tailtrod led her to a more secluded, private area. They stopped at a door that had mouse-guards outside it, and the Captain spoke to them. They shot through a crack in the double door, which after a few moments parted slightly to allow entry.

"The king." Tailtrod announced pompously.

Clara went in.

It was empty.

There was a long, human-sized dining table with chairs running down the length of the room, and a great fire burned in a hefty stone hearth at the far end. The grey walls were reflected in the dark mahogany table, making the space appear cramped and gloomy, despite the torches and the fire and the large window, from which the dense snow outside glowed inwards. Clara waited, distinctly unimpressed, the only sound being the crackling coming from the flames.

"So this is the girl who brought the traitor to me."

Clara jumped, and looked at the floor, for that was where the miniature monarch would enter, and she wanted to look him defiantly in the eyes before he handed down his sentence. She heard footsteps, which initially she thought were far too heavy to be that of a mouse, but then again, perhaps in his gluttony the king was overweight. She kept her eyes fixed on the floor, just in front of her feet.

A few seconds later, she heard an ominous chuckle. "Look at me, child."

Confused, Clara raised her head.

And then she understood everything, for she was looking at The Mouse King, and The Mouse King was a human.

CHAPTER TEN
ESCAPE

It all made sense now. The reason why the mice lived in a grand castle, why they had taught themselves to adapt to larger proportions. Their king was not a mouse.

And Clara felt afraid.

It was clear to her now that she would be outmatched, for The Mouse King was tall and towered above her, in a similar way to how she towered above Bertram. He cut an intimidating figure; a long, storm-grey coat with tails hung down over a silken berry-red waistcoat, ivory breeches and flat black shoes. Protruding from the neck of his coat were several stiff feathers, which were tall and black with a greenish sheen, and they created a high, regal collar about his shoulders. But worst of all was his countenance, for he had no human face. Instead he wore a giant helmet that rendered his human self unidentifiable and gave him the appearance of a grotesque, hideous mouse. Cast in silver and covering the entirety of his head, including his hair, it was a disgusting display of vanity and perversion. Rounded metal ears, each as wide as a dinner plate, stuck out from either side of his head, and there were no nose or mouth holes but simply an elongated metal snout that protruded from the centre of the helmet, complete with a false nose and wire whiskers, each of which was at least a meter long. The only openings in the disguise were where the eyes would be, and even these had been disturbingly enlarged, so that they swallowed up the real human eyes within and Clara found herself gazing at two bottomless pits. The eyes were shaped in such a way that the mask looked as if it were perpetually glaring, and emotion lines had been etched onto the forehead so that the glare became one of evil, cruel, triumph.

This was no king of rodents. This was a demon, masquerading as one.

He sat down at the head of the table. "Come." The voice from within the mask was distorted, and Clara had to concentrate to make it out.

Unnerved, she tiptoed forward only the tiniest of inches, but The Mouse King nodded his approval. She herself dared not speak, and it was quiet for a few minutes before the king began.

"Do you know why you are here?"

"Yes."

"You are here because you have something, correct? Something I want."

Clara couldn't hold back her fear any longer. "Please don't hurt Bertram! He hasn't done anything; only be a little timid, which, where I come from, is a very admirable trait in any mouse! Please! We are not traitors, we have done nothing to cause you upset, we –"

The Mouse King held up a black-gloved hand. "That is not what I meant. Yes, the turncoat will be dealt with accordingly, but later, after we have done business." He sat back, observing her. "You have something very valuable to me. Something in your jacket."

Clara was baffled. Surely he couldn't mean...?

"This?" asked Clara, pulling out the nutcracker.

Upon seeing it, The Mouse King let out a gratified sigh, as if it brought him much pleasure. "Yes. That. At last."

"What is it to you? How do you know of it?" Clara hated the nutcracker, but that didn't mean that she was willing to give it to a fearful enemy without question.

"I know more about it than you ever could." The Mouse King said bluntly. "Listen to me, girl child. That nutcracker has something very special of mine locked away inside of it. To open it, I need your help. I have tried to open it many times myself, but I cannot. Your intense emotions and personal connections to it, however, make you a perfect key."

"Why would I ever help a tyrant?"

"To save your friends from death, of course." He leaned forward. "Help me retrieve what is mine, everything will return to the way it was."

Clara's guard was still up, but she heard herself asking: "And how would I do that?"

He leaned forward. "My subjects might be stupid, but I am not. I know that you are not from this Plane. I know that you invoked The Clock-Stop Curse, therefore I know that you are trying to get to The Land of Light, the place that grants wishes and your heart's delight."

"So?"

"So it would seem that we both have a wish, no? You can help me achieve mine. Allow me to escort you into The Land of Light, and when that nutcracker opens, what is contained within it will be mine."

"How can anything be contained in here? It's solid wood."

"Such an ignorant, foolish little human. After everything you'd seen tonight I thought you'd readily agree that, sometimes, some things really are beyond explanation."

Clara toyed with the nutcracker. "I don't trust you. I have no reason to."

"And quite rightly so. But the lives of your friends hang in the balance; can you really afford to gamble with them?"

"If I unleash what is in here, they could be as good as dead anyway."

When he next spoke, The Mouse King's voice took on a surprising sincerity. "I swear to you, what is contained inside that figure is benign. I know others have a tendency to paint me and the mice as cold-blooded killers, but the reality is that I rule my kingdom firmly and justly. I'm not a bad person Clara. Just... misunderstood."

Clara gazed downward. "I would like to return to my cell. To have some time to think about things."

"As you wish." declared the king. He called for Captain Tailtrod, who came at once to escort Clara back to the dungeon. After she had slid the nutcracker back into her pocket, she curtseyed to the king and turned to leave, Tailtrod pointing his staff at her heels.

"Oh, and by the way." called The Mouse King after her.

Clara spun on her heel to look at him again.

"I know you're a clever girl, but whatever you do, don't try to outsmart me. Remember, I can kill both you and your friends with just a single order." With that, he waved her away.

It was a long, unforgiving march back to the prison, and Clara felt sick with fear and apprehension. If she fulfilled The Mouse King's request, then who knew what terror she could set free? On the other hand, if she didn't, she and her friends would probably die the most horrible, painful deaths imaginable.

As soon as Tailtrod had locked her back into her cell, Bertram and Shiverfinger came running over.

"Finally! Are you alright? What did he want?"

Clara blinked; it took her a few seconds to adjust to the darkness after being in the cold light of upstairs. "I'm fine. He wants to come with us to The Land of Light. There's something inside of the nutcracker, something he's desperate for, that only I can release when I get there. If I don't agree... we all die."

In the dark, she felt Bertram's paw grasp her wrist earnestly. "Listen." His voice was low and urgent. "You cannot give into him."

"I know. I –"

"Our lives don't matter. If the king gets his hands on that thing, whatever it is, there's no telling what he could do."

"Which is why —"

"You really have to think about the bigger picture!"

"Can I speak?" Clara hissed. "I know I can't let him have what's inside the nutcracker. But I'm pretty intent on not dying as well. Which is why... which is why we have to escape."

For a moment, Bertram seemed to be rendered speechless, which was quite an impressive feat in itself. "Escape?" he stammered. "From Mausburg?"

"Yes."

"And how do you suppose we do that?"

"I'm not sure... but rock can't be that much different from snow, right?" Clara winked at him and went to stand in front of the prison cell wall.

"Stilton's breath." muttered Bertram as he moved to one side.

Clara tried to focus. In her mind's eye she imagined the stone simply crumbling away as if it were dry sand. "The wall will fall." she declared. She saw it collapsing, vanishing under the might of her power. "The wall will fall. The wall will fall!"

Slowly, she opened her eyes. The rock had not shed so much as a single pebble. Clara groaned and walked away from the wall. They were trapped.

"So... what now?" Bertram asked hesitantly.

Clara didn't answer, mainly because she didn't have one. Their only option now left them literally stuck between a rock and hard place.

She had failed them. Bertram, Shiverfinger, even Uncle Drosselmeyer. She had failed them all. She had nothing left to fight for now, and if the king decided to kill her, then so be it. Better to die than rot in this cell, where she would never be free again.

She felt Bertram scurry into her hand as Shiverfinger flew over. "Don't give up hope, Clara! Remember, The Land of Light is built on imagination and belief! So, believe!"

Clara choked on a sob. "I'm not sure I can."

"I believe in you, pretty fairy." Shiverfinger said consolingly.

"Me too. It's just like before." Bertram added.

Glancing at her friends, Clara got to her feet with an exhausted sigh. She would do this. She had to do this.

Focusing hard on the wall, she began to concentrate. Maybe it wasn't what she was doing, but rather how she was going about it. Maybe she needed better words, something like the incantation that had started The Clock-Stop Curse in the first place.

She thought for a moment or two, concentrating, as Bertram and Shiverfinger watched her intently. Eventually, she came up with something. It was short and simple, and it wasn't the best, but maybe it would do the trick. Clara closed her eyes and focused on the rocks again.

"Crack and crumble, weakened wall, let yourself give way and fall!"

Suddenly, without warning, a massive explosion rocked her, and with a cry, she fell forward. As the ringing in her ears subsided and the shockwave evaporated, she sat up and looked around.

Moonlight, pure and clear, now flooded the dungeon. A huge hole had appeared in the rear wall of her cell, and when she looked at it, she could see the smoky clouds of night billowing past on the other side. Shaken, Clara staggered to her feet and looked at Shiverfinger, who was stood by the newly-formed chasm. Clara knew that, for as long as she lived, she'd never see anything as beautiful as the fractals in the ice sprite's skin shimmering under the full, free moon.

"Well that worked!" Clara cried jubilantly, but inside she was shaken. Where was this power coming from?

"This is a very noisy escape plan." noted Bertram as Shiverfinger tried to lift the fallen rubble out of their way. "The mouse legion could always come back, you know."

Clara swallowed. "I know." She had hoped that the dungeons were too far away for anyone in the keep to hear them, but Bertram was right; she was flirting with danger and she knew it, but worrying wasn't going to help anyone. Instead, she buried her nerves and called up to the ice sprite: "Shiverfinger, get us out of here, now! Bertram, get inside my jumper!"

As if on cue, the sound of the mouse legion cascading down the steps echoed towards them, the Captain shouting out orders as they went.

"Told you they'd be back." Bertram slipped down Clara's collar, out of sight. Glancing backwards, she saw Captain Tailtrod clambering up the door, fumbling with his keys.

"You stay right where you are!" he bellowed.

But though he might have thought he was fast, he was nowhere near as quick as an ice sprite crafted from the magic of Father Winter. With the swiftness of a rapid-flowing river, Shiverfinger dipped down, gathered Clara up in his arms, and flew out of the opening just as the Captain managed to open the door.

"No!" he shrieked. "Stop them!"

But it was too late. By the time reinforcements had arrived and The Mouse King had been summoned, the fugitives had long gone.

Surveying the damage, the monarch was furious. His human height made him seem like a great, formidable titan to his army.

"Find them!" he screeched at Captain Tailtrod. "All of you; get out there in the snow, and find them, quickly! Take them alive, or dead if you must – the fugitives do not matter, but I want that nutcracker!"

CHAPTER ELEVEN
SOMMERGRAS

"Remind me of the route again?"
Bertram yelled over the noise of the wind.

"Walk along this western crag, up past the
highest peak, down the steepest slope below and
across the fields bleak! Although I think we
circumnavigated most of that thanks to your old
employer."

"Well, I'd certainly say we're over the
fields bleak!" grumbled the mouse.

Clara didn't argue with him. Cradled in Shiverfinger's arms, at high altitude, in the middle of something that threatened to develop into a blizzard, she felt deeply worried. She would actually have preferred to be back on the ground again, for at least there she was in control of herself. As it was, now she was subjected to Shiverfinger's energetic flying, and she could only cough, splutter and blink as the heavily-falling snow smacked her in the face.

"How's the nutcracker? she asked Bertram.

She felt him wriggling around inside her coat. It tickled, but a few minutes later he reappeared. "All good. Still secure. Why is it so important, anyway?"

"I don't know, but I'm going to find out."
said Clara determinedly. Then she put her head
down against Shiverfinger's chest and tried to
protect herself from the barrage of oncoming
snow. They had to get to The Fortress of
Forgotten Things soon; otherwise she would
never see her mother and Ferdy ever again.
Distractedly, she thought of them, frozen in time
back home, where the party was probably still a
roaring success. If they could see her now, they'd
never believe it, but she missed them terribly.

Suddenly, Shiverfinger gave an almighty
screech of warning and dove. Clara could barely
scream as the wind whipped past her face as they
plummeted, the cold, expansive ground rushing
up towards them. Her mind whirled; was it The

Mouse King's army, come to find them already? Would they take them back to Mausburg and inflict a whole variety of tortuous punishments on them until they actually begged to die? Clara felt sick at the thought.

Mind you, she didn't feel any less sick if she concentrated on the present moment, for now Shiverfinger was swerving and ducking beneath clutches of trees as he flew low to the ground, trying to throw off whoever it was that pursued them. His speed nauseated Clara, and even when he stopped, landing in the snow and setting her down next to a thick fallen log as cover, her stomach took more than a few minutes to settle.

"Pretty fairy stay." he instructed her, and then slunk away, into the forest.

"Shiverfinger!" Clara cried. "Wait!"

But he had already stepped so far forward into the mist that surrounded them that he was now nothing more than a hazy outline. He continued with the greatest care, his tread delicate, as he sought out whatever it was that had caused them to stop out of necessity. And then, when the distance in between them became so far that Shiverfinger almost seemed to be merely a smudge on the wintry landscape, Clara could only watch as he leapt at someone, knocking them to the ground with shocking force.

The sound that followed reminded Clara of the noises cats made when fighting; eerie sounds that echoed loudly all across the tundra.

"Stop, please!" a delicate, feminine voice cried from afar.

Stunned, Clara forgot all thoughts of danger to herself and ran towards the commotion.

What she saw was not what she expected. For there, in a clearing under the trees, was Shiverfinger, ferociously and unrelentingly pinning another form to the ground, but it was not a mouse, nor a human.

It was a minute woman, about two feet tall, and she was as slender and graceful as Shiverfinger himself. Also like Shiverfinger, she had striking, opalescent wings, which flicked and twitched in a myriad of colour as she tried to wriggle free of the foot that was pressed squarely into the middle of her back. In every other regard however, she was so unlike the ice sprite that they were polar opposites. She had human-like skin, which, though pale, had a rosy glow and shone with the sheen of a million dewdrops. Her hair, which was the colour of freshly-ripened wheat, was scraped back into a tight bun, and atop her head was a fragile wreath of pink and yellow buds. Though she was barefoot, she was clothed, wearing a knee-length dress that was made out of dusky petals; smaller around the strapless bodice but much larger in the skirt, which flared out slightly at the hips and hem. She looked full of warmth and grace… which is why it stunned Clara that Shiverfinger was snarling and growling at her as if she would do them great harm.

"Shiverfinger, let her go!" Clara shouted.

"Please! I mean no mischief!" pleaded the beautiful being. Her voice was as musical as church bells on a sunny morning.

"She followed us!" complained Shiverfinger.

"Well then, let us see what she has to say." said Clara sagely, with a look that commanded the ice sprite do as he was told.

With a sigh, Shiverfinger removed his foot and stepped away. The slight woman coughed in relief, and then scrambled to her feet.

"My name is Glimmerwing. Your friend here has flown you into flower fae territory."

"I'm sorry." Clara started to explain. "We didn't realise this was anyone's domain. We were just passing through."

Glimmerwing shook her head. "That's not what I mean. I was letting you know you will be safe here. You see, I have just come from the east – visiting friends at Lovers' Lake – and I had to fly over Mausburg. I heard gossip, and saw much. The king is in a dreadful rage; he's amassing his armies, ordering them to search the wastelands for fugitives. When I saw you flying up there, I wondered if you might be them, so I came to offer my assistance and let you know that The Mouse King has a warrant out for your arrest. You must be quite important to him, whoever you are."

"I'm not surprised. We've upset him quite a bit tonight. I'm Clara, he's Shiverfinger and this... is Bertram." Clara finished as the latter appeared on her palm.

Upon seeing him, the flower fae blanched in horror and bewilderment.

"Please." begged Bertram. "I know what you're thinking. But I swear to you, none of us have any allegiance to or love for The Mouse King, especially me."

"I'm sorry, but the word of a whiskered one holds no merit as far as I'm concerned. But you – Clara – I like you. There's honesty in your eyes. If I am to let you into the realm of my people, as I want to do, I must ensure that it is safe. Is what he says true?"

"Yes. There is a way to defeat our enemies. We just have to get to The Fortress of Forgotten Things."

"And what, pray tell, could a human, mouse and ice sprite need in such a place?"

"The path to The Land of Light."

Glimmerwing studied Clara for a moment before nodding. "Of course, of course. The Clock-Stop Curse is the only way a human can enter The Hinterworld."

"We were following the directions Shiverfinger was given by Father Winter, but now I think we're lost thanks to The Mouse King's intervening." Clara clarified.

"Not lost. Just off course. I myself lead the flower fae; perhaps we can help you. It's surrounded by a magic spell; you'll never get through on your own."

"Thank you. Please forgive our frayed nerves; we've been heavily persecuted and it's been a long night."

"Quite alright. I understand entirely." She turned and put her hand out towards Shiverfinger. "I am sorry if I scared you." she said simply. "You and your friends will be safe now. I promise."

Shiverfinger didn't say anything, but he shook her hand and gave her a shy smile before going and standing behind Clara for protection.

Glimmerwing turned and addressed the group as one. "I will take you to the Fortress myself if necessary; this doesn't need to become more of a suicide mission than it apparently already has been. Plus, if you can do whatever it is you say you need to, it sounds like there's a chance those flea-bitten vermin might stop trampling everything that belongs to the fae. Come this way."

She set off at a stride into the forest. She might have been small and delicate, but the pace at which she was going made it quite apparent that she wasn't going to slow down for any stragglers, and so Clara charged on right behind her, watching her step as she trudged through the snow, Father Winter's boots and gloves staying true to their purpose.

"Shiverfinger was so fierce towards her. I'm surprised she gave us help at all!" Clara quietly fretted to Bertram as the caravan of misfits headed along the trail.

"Don't worry. Spring and winter have always quarrelled, ever since the dawn of time." he told her. "They're always at odds with each other, so what happened back there is nothing new, and none of your fault. Old rivalries die hard."

Clara nodded. She had no interest in getting involved in petty, centuries-old squabbles. All she wanted to do was to set the clocks going again and make everything right.

She resolved to keep her head down from now on, and try not to consciously further upset the status quo of The Hinterworld.

It wasn't long until they came to a thick mossy embankment that was several feet high. To Clara, it looked like a defensive outer wall; it had a dense, wooden portcullis at the entrance, and tiny windows peeped out of the thick vegetation, which sprawled all over the impressive barrier. It was also surprisingly free of snow. Of course; snowflakes would never dare to land on the home of the magical beings who were the embodiment of spring and summer. Clara was also sure that, from somewhere on the other side, she could hear beautiful music in the air; the sound of panpipes and flutes; the sound of joy one might find on a June or July evening. It looked astonishing; an eternal green haven amidst the never-ending palette of white, black and grey.

Glimmerwing stepped up to the portcullis, and a sentry went forwards to the gate to meet her, looking out at them with fearful eyes.

"Relax, Elvenear." the fae leader decreed with a calm-yet-authoritative voice that Clara was sure had developed after many years of gaining respect. "I bring guests to Sommergras."

The sentry, who was wearing a helmet fashioned from acorns, nodded deeply and, with force and strength, pulled on a cord at the side of the gate. Gradually, the portcullis rose, and Glimmerwing stepped through and indicated that the others should do the same, even though Clara had to duck quite low; as a result, she felt grossly cumbersome, like a giant in a folktale.

What was presented to them was a large, lush square that formed the basis of a fae village. It was surrounded by oak trees that, despite the frigid weather beyond, still held onto their summer coats as if the breeze that blew in over the ramparts was of no concern to them, the strings of warm twinkling lights hanging from their branches illuminating the night sky. In amongst the trees were buildings that were six feet high at most; shops and cafés made from beautifully smoothed wood complete with quaint verandas, with their wares – which varied from clothing made from plant matter to glass vials containing mysterious things for spells and such – displayed proudly on their porches, their amber lamps glowing brightly at their windows. In the centre of the square itself was a huge maypole, around which a noisy crowd of flower fae danced as a small orchestra stood by and played the instruments Clara had heard earlier. Some other fae went about their business, not stopping to join in the festivities but hurrying down the paths that led off from the square and onto the domiciliary areas of the settlement. To Clara, Sommergras felt very much like an old frontier town, as if it were the last stronghold of civilisation in an empty and unforgiving wilderness.

Clara drunk everything in, and as she did Glimmerwing cast an appreciative eye up at her. "It's beautiful, yes?"

"I can't believe everything you've done here."

"We had to survive, somehow. The flower fae are a dying breed." Their leader looked about her and saw a rose that was wilting in a nearby patch of wildflowers. For a moment, she seemed disturbed – and then she put her hand to it. The trio of friends watched, dumbfounded, as, in a shower of light, the rose grew, its stem straightened and it stood proud again. Glimmerwing giggled and winked back at them.

"You have magic?" asked Bertram incredulously.

"Of course!" she chuckled. "Father Winter is not the only one who can make wonders. Unfortunately, no doubt if you've already met him you'll know that he is a little... utilitarian. How I wish you had come to us first! Us fae could have shown you where there is real joy to be had in magic."

"I understand that. But we really don't have time for joy. We must get to the Land of Light." Clara was getting frustrated with everyone speaking in riddles again.

"I made you a promise, didn't I?" demanded Glimmerwing. "A flower fae never breaks their promise! But humans – why, humans are so impatient it is unforgivable. You stopped the clocks, and still you have no time!"

Saying no more but leaving Clara to feel incredibly guilty, Glimmerwing flew over to a nearby balcony that was built into a thick old tree at the head of the square. None of the other fae paid her much attention, leading Clara to wonder how she was going to get it amidst all the noise of the revelry. Then, as if she had been waiting for a cue, Glimmerwing lifted her arms high into the air and began to wave her hands. A shower of golden sparks shot from her fingers like a firework, crackling in the air up above and drawing all the glances of those who had not paid heed to her.

"Good fae of Sommergras! For centuries now, we have kept our stronghold safe against The Hinterworld's never-ending winter, making sure that the magic of the flower fae cannot be vanquished by the forces that naturally seek to destroy it. That war is the way of the world. However, recently, we have found a new foe in our midst. I do not need to say to whom I refer."

There was some murmuring in the crowd at this, some nodding of heads and noises of agreement. Everyone, it seemed, was fed up with the mice. Glimmerwing continued:

"As you know, we have tried many times to find a way to defend ourselves against these relentless hordes, but we cannot. Yet, as I was flying back from Lovers' Lake and patrolling the woods outside our borders, I came across some people who think they may be able to help us.

Their names are Clara, Shiverfinger and Bertram."

When the flower fae turned as one and saw exactly who this aid consisted of, there were gasps of astounded bewilderment.

"An ice sprite and a mouse? Both our enemies together? How? Why?" cried one fae adamantly.

"Sommergras will never be safe again!" lamented another.

"Believe me, friends!" Glimmerwing shouted over the rising din. "I was as hesitant to bring them here as you are to let them stay now, but they are wanted by The Mouse King, with such intensity that I do not doubt their claim that they have a way to triumph over him. So we would do well not to delay their journey."

"What do they need from us?" asked a round fae man.

"I'm glad you asked kind sir! They need safe passage to The Fortress of Forgotten Things. From there, they will be able to reach The Land of Light – or so their leader assures me."

"But that's such a long way! So cold, so terrible, so unforgiving!" A woman holding two flower fae babies settled them on her hip. "We can't send them away!"

"Quite right we can't, Violetdew! Which is exactly why we must help them!" From across the crowd, Glimmerwing locked eyes with Clara;

her eyes were alight with mirth. "It is why we must do some magic!"

At this, an almighty gasp went around the square.

"We can break the spell!" cried a fae – and suddenly all the others were volunteering, becoming a mass of squeaking voices.

After a few minutes of this Glimmerwing motioned for them to settle. "Of course we can!" she told them happily. "It will take all our strength, but of course we can!"

"And then they go again and we are safe and secret once more!"

"Even better than that!" Glimmerwing added. "The Mouse King will be defeated!"

"No more mouse king!"

"Let's go now!"

"We can help the strange ones –"

"– who will bring about our freedom!"

A great cheer went up then, like a wave crashing on the shore, and suddenly all the flower fae clamoured around Clara, Bertram and Shiverfinger, calling out their names and shouting goodwill messages in a sea of reaching hands and smiling faces.

Despite the chaos, Clara found herself giggling, for the joy of the fae was infectious. She reached for their hands, being gracious to them in return, and suddenly realised that this must be akin to something a hero might feel. Someone at the back came forward with a small plate of cheese and proffered it to Bertram, who didn't need to be asked twice before he dove head-long into the dairy. Shiverfinger, as was his way, didn't say much, but he took it all in his stead and actually seemed bemused by the beings who were so different from him and yet so similar, almost as if he were comparing his frosty, icy grace to their warm, floral beauty.

Eventually, the flower fae remembered the task at hand, and with a call from Glimmerwing they flooded the gate to Sommergras, so that poor Elvenear had to hoist up the portcullis and keep it open for a more considerable amount of time than normal. And just like that, the inhabitants of the fae stronghold were out and free in the forest, flying amongst the trees and crying out in jubilation, creating eerie whoops of noise that made Clara think that all those stories she'd heard as a child about fairies haunting forests might not necessarily be false.

Just as she realised that she was struggling to keep up with the fluttering fae on her average human legs, she felt someone lift her and the ground come away from under her feet. Tilting her head, she looked up and saw Shiverfinger, holding her under her arms and flying determinedly.

"Hold tight pretty fairy." he reassured her. "You go home soon."

"Thank you Shiverfinger." she said with gratitude in her voice. "Throughout this whole journey, you have been a most excellent guardian."

And so, as the flower fae of Sommergras braced themselves to face much colder climates, Clara Stahlbaum vanished into the night once again.

CHAPTER TWELVE
THE DANCE OF
THE FLOWER FAE

The flower fae landed on the dunes of snow as gently as dandelion seeds, with Shiverfinger depositing Clara just as carefully alongside them. There was no sound but the howling wind, and the atmosphere was one that only fallen snow creates.

There was no doubt in Clara's mind that these were the fields bleak that Shiverfinger had spoken of. Great hills of snow almost as tall as Clara reached up towards the sky, turning the landscape into an eerie, twisted desert. Suddenly, she was very grateful to have the fae of Sommergras alongside her. She squinted as she looked out over the vast wasteland, and as she did, she saw in the distance four pointed turrets reaching into the thick cloud cover, like icicles that had been broken off and then turned upside down.

Bertram appeared at the neck of her jumper. "That's it! That's The Fortress of Forgotten Things!"

Clara didn't need him to tell her. She already knew. It was akin to the feeling she got when she returned to Sweetmeadow Place. Something about that building was calling to her, and as she looked at its distant, ice-clad spectre, she felt her throat constrict. This was it. She would set things right, and then she would go home.

She turned to Glimmerwing at the side of her, and, with calm authority in her voice, told her: "Whatever you're going to do, do it now. Please; before anything else happens or The Mouse King catches up with us."

Glimmerwing nodded deeply. Then, standing tall at the head of the army of flower fae, she cast her arms up into the air, making graceful, slow motions with her hands, as if she were commanding the air to do her bidding. The other flower fae, who could see their leader stood at the crest of the dune, followed her lead and copied her, and before long, bright, brilliant sparks, golden and amber in their hues, filled the bitter air, which turned warmer as the glowing orbs of light multiplied. Bertram's nose twitched as he caught the scent of strawberries being carried by on a summery breeze.

Clara looked about her in wonder, for now the flower fae were not only moving their arms but their entire bodies. Glimmerwing, who in the enchanted light would have captured a mortal's heart instantly, pointed her toes and sashayed, keeping in time with a spritely jig only she could seem to hear. The sparks she had created danced all around her, encircling her arms, hair and legs; it was almost like she was playing with them, as if she gained sheer joy from their presence. Clara looked over her shoulder and saw that the other fae were doing the same, willing the orbs of lights they had created to dance in time with their ethereal movements, to swirl and flow on rivers of air so that eventually all the sparks filled the night sky with their glow. This dancing and merrymaking and joyful creating continued for a long while, until Clara and her companions were illuminated by the warming radiance of the magical orbs, and there were more of them than there were shining stars in the heavens.

Then, with one final, grand wave, Glimmerwing used her magic to gather up all the sparkling lights, and sent them cascading onto the snowdrifts below.

The orbs were imbued with the magic of spring and summer. Thoughts of sunshine, beach waves and short, moonlit nights were the composition of their very essence. When they looked upon the snow, it should have trembled. When they touched the frozen gate, it should have opened.

But the orbs did not. For when they touched the entrance to The Fortress of Forgotten Things, a mighty, unseen force simply bounced the warm magic back towards the fae at breakneck speed.

There were noises of alarm as their magic shot back towards them, meaning those on the frontline – including Clara – had to move quickly to get out of the way of the reverberating enchantment. The orbs landed amongst the ranks, dissipating into explosions of butterflies and sunbeams as they hit the nearby ground and trees.

But not one of them had made a way through.

As the fae lamented over what to do next, Clara looked out once more at the fortress. It was right there. After all this journeying, the key to stopping The Clock-Stop Curse, the key to The Land of Light and the key to making everything right again was right there... but it was barricaded, by snow and magic.

Clara made up her mind. "Come on Bertram." she told her friend. Before anyone could stop her, she started down the sloping snowdrift.

"Clara, wait! It's too dangerous!" she heard Glimmerwing protest.

But Clara wasn't listening. She had to keep going. She had to make it right. Father Winter had given her boots and gloves that meant her feet and fingers would never get cold, The Mouse King had made her brave, and the flower fae had shown her the way. Now it was up to her. So she trudged forward through the depths of snow that no mortal should have been able to tread, and even though it was almost up to her knees and her cheeks were red with the bite of cold, she kept going.

"Clara, stop!" Glimmerwing called out.

No. I don't want to stop, thought Clara as she closed her eyes. *I want to go forward.*

With an enormous whoosh, the waves of snow withdrew from Clara as if they were on a retreating tide, clearing the way and enabling her to step forward onto solid ground. The flower fae gasped behind her, but Clara didn't let that deter her as she imagined the snow simply drifting away; all of it, right up to the entrance to The Fortress of Forgotten Things.

The whooshing stopped. Clara opened her eyes.

The field before her was clear, as if it was spring.

With an elated smile, Clara looked back over her shoulder towards Glimmerwing, who was staring at her with an open mouth, and the other fae looked just as stunned. Their leader drifted down towards Clara on her gossamer wings.

"No human has ever..." she began.

"I know." finished Clara.

"How?"

"I don't know, but I'm hoping that whatever's in there will have all the answers."

Glimmerwing nodded. "Then go well, Clara." she said, and gave the girl a sticky kiss on her forehead.

Smiling back at her, Clara set off, Shiverfinger following her up above.

Relief flooded her when she finally reached the entrance to the Fortress. It looked just like it had in the vision of her father; a fort made completely out of crystalline ice, the turrets disappearing into the clouds, and a door that was so solid it looked as if it needed multiple men to lift it.

Clara's heart was thudding so loud that it sounded like a grandfather clock. If she got this wrong... no, that wasn't going to happen. She steeled herself.

"Alright Bertram, let's do this." There was no twitch at her jumper sleeve in response, no scurry at her neckline. "Bertram?"

She looked down at the ground. The mouse was stood there, ears drooping and tail low, looking infinitely sad.

Clara crouched down to him. "Bertram? What's wrong?"

"This is the last time I'll ever see the outdoors." he said resignedly.

"What are you talking about? We'll come out of this, I promise you."

"Not me. Clara, this is The Fortress of Forgotten Things; the things that are lost, that no one wants any more, that no one remembers. Everything the Planes don't want is here, because people forgot about them. Things like broken toys, bad memories... and a cowardly mouse who deserted his legion."

"What? Bertram, no, no! That is not true! You don't have to stay here! You don't belong here!"

He let out a little non-humorous laugh. "It's alright Clara. I made my mind up long before you came. It'll be a quiet life. I won't have to fight again. I can be a mouse again! My only wish is that more people were like you, so that they were able to see the good in everybody. Thank you for seeing the good in me."

He shuffled off towards the entrance. Clara watched him go, ready to consign himself to a life of nothingness. Her heart pulled and tugged and twisted, until suddenly she shouted:

"Get back here, mouse! Don't you dare abandon your legion a second time!"

Bertram stopped and turned around. "What?"

"I said, get back here! Your legion needs you." She gestured to herself and Shiverfinger. "I thought we were in this together, for safe passage in one navy jumper until we got to where we were going!"

Upon hearing this, Bertram finally understood, and his face broke into a wide grin. He ran as fast as he could on all fours towards Clara, his red waistcoat flapping, and leapt from the ground into her awaiting palm, where she lifted him up to her cheek and held him close.

"I remember you." she whispered to him. "I care about you. Bertram, I wouldn't want to be without you ever again. Now, let's go and make everything good and right, together, okay?"

Shiverfinger sidled up alongside them. "We go now?"

Clara looked up at the building that disappeared into the sky. Tentatively, she took a step forward towards the Fortress. The dense ice door that graced its face swung back on its thick rivets with a shudder, almost as if it was being pulled back by the hand of a phantom. Releasing a breath she didn't know she held, Clara answered her friend.

"Yes Shiverfinger. We go now."

CHAPTER THIRTEEN
MEMORIES

It was dark in the Fortress of Forgotten Things. Not in the way that nights are dark, or woods, or murky water. It was dark in the way that human souls turn dark after they've kept a terrible secret for too long, or dark in the way that tongues are supposed to turn after a person has told a lie that they know will bring unhappiness to many. It was even darker than Mausburg had been.

"So... what are we actually looking for in here? Considering we can't actually see anything." Bertram asked reasonably.

"I don't know. Right now I'm just following my gut."

"Y'know, my gut's never been of use to me in my life."

"That's because yours is telling you it's always hungry!"

"Pretty fairy make right decision. I trust pretty fairy." Shiverfinger added sagely.

"Thank you Shiv-" Clara was cut off as she lost her footing and slipped in the darkness, yelping as she did.

"Yeah... maybe pretty fairy should try magicking us some light before we all get ourselves killed?"

"Oh, shut up Bertram." hissed Clara, but she did as she was told. She imagined a glowing ball of light, similar to the ones the flower fae had created, leading the way in front of her. When she opened her eyes, there it was.

Now that the way before her was illuminated, Clara looked around at the interior walls of the Fortress. They were not icy as she expected, but lined with wood. She walked over to them, the light bobbing slightly above her head, and as she gave them a closer inspection, Clara realised the truth.

Wooden chests were stacked high against the wintry walls, filled with the forgotten things Bertram had been talking about. Reaching right to the ceiling of the Fortress, there were a whole manner of sad objects; a marionette with snapped strings, a handheld mirror with its glass smashed and even missing in places, pairs of trousers with holes in them and skirts with fraying stitching. They weren't even stored properly or locked away in case the person who had once cared about these things might come back to reclaim them. They had simply been discarded and left to rot.

"How on Earth could the key to The Land of Light be in here?" Clara wondered aloud incredulously. This was no mystical cave of wonders; this was a universe's junk shop. She was starting to feel vaguely disturbed by all that she was seeing, and it left her on edge; especially when she passed a porcelain doll with its painted face caved in, a clown puppet with half its hair torn off or an old black-and-white photograph of a baby in dated clothes. This was no fortress of things that were forgotten; this is where hope went to die and nightmares were created.

While it nauseated Clara, it did seem fitting that her Papa had led her to a place such as this. As she had said many a time, her hope had died when he did, and no matter how much she tried to deny it, living without him was a waking nightmare too.

Despite Father Winter's boots and gloves, Clara suddenly felt very cold indeed.

"What matter, pretty fairy?" Shiverfinger asked her.

She smiled back at him kindly, trying to ease his childlike conscious. "Oh, nothing." she assured him before going back to her searching. She tried desperately to remember if her vision had shown her anything, if the apparition of her father had led her to something, but all she could recall was him walking into the wide open entryway of the building and being swallowed up by it, never to come back out.

They kept on moving forwards, but what towards, they had no idea. The broken objects that covered the ground alongside them did nothing to cheer their mood, but Clara reasoned that the Fortress had to come to an end eventually, and that when she reached that end, she might find a passageway that would lead her to The Land of Light.

She was just figuring out what she would do if that were the case, when she saw something that made her body, heart and soul stop still.

There, draped over a white wooden chair, was a small pink tutu that glimmered and glittered. Its bodice was adorned with lace panelling and pearls, while the skirt was decorated with silver sequins and pink satin rosebuds. On the floor, beneath the chair, was a pair of pink pointé shoes, just waiting to be tied to the feet of an avid and enthusiastic student.

As if she were in a trance, Clara went over to the outfit. Shiverfinger and Bertram bestowed her with querying glances, but she paid no attention to them. She picked the tutu up, hugging it to her chest.

She remembered.

It was twelve days before Christmas. Clara was so excited she could barely breathe.

Not just for Christmas, of course, but for the fact that tonight, she would be playing the role of the sugarplum fairy in her ballet school's winter performance. She had trained years for this moment, and now, at the grand age of twelve, it was finally her time. Tonight, even though she was by no means the eldest dancer at the school, or the prettiest, she was the sugarplum fairy.

She had wanted her whole family to come and
bear witness to her proudest moment – Uncle
Drosselmeyer, her Germanic relatives, maybe her cousins
and of course Pyotr – but as it was she was only allowed
to reserve three tickets, so only Papa, Mama and Ferdy
were coming. A comparatively scaled-down affair, but
lovely nonetheless.

Under the dressing room lighting, her tutu
sparkled like magic. It was the best tutu in the school's
wardrobe, with lace, pearls, sequins and satin roses, and
tonight, she got to wear it and have her hair scraped back
into a tight bun and pink twinkly shadow on her eyelids,
because tonight it was her turn.

Her friend Lucy shuffled past her, preening herself
and applying more lipstick in the Hollywood-style mirror

next to where Clara sat, not doing anything for fear of smudging her own makeup.

"It's filling up out there." she said, and she turned her head away from her ablutions to share an excited, thrilled grin with Clara. "Are you nervous?"

"A little."

"Don't be. You'll be fine."

Suddenly, their dance teacher called them to the stage and in a flurry of hairspray and glitter they accumulated in the wings. Clara waited patiently in the shadows – she wouldn't go on until the final act, but she liked to watch the others and congratulate them when they returned backstage.

Her parents would be out there, she knew, with Ferdy shuffling impatiently next to them and begging for sweets. Idly, she wondered what flowers Papa would have

put in his bouquet. She hoped it was roses. She loved
roses.

As the first few dancers twirled onto the theatre,
Clara found herself swept up in the magic of the moment.
The stage, performing like this, was where she truly
belonged. When the music reached its crescendo and she
was sure no one was looking, she crept forward and went
to go and get a better look at the audience.

They were rapt and attentive. Really, she wasn't
surprised; the school had gone all out with its production
this year. There were cardboard cut-outs of sweets,
Christmas trees and flowers. The audience were
enchanted.

There was just one problem.
Her family wasn't there.

Clara immediately grew troubled. Her parents had never missed a performance, not one, even when she had been very small and played embarrassing and non-important roles like 'Third Sheep'. There was no way they would miss her big performance, especially not when she was the sugarplum fairy.

Clara cast a worried glance at the stage. It was the turn of some boys that were dancing as gingerbread men, and she was next.

Then, before she could feign sickness or nerves or anything else that might have bought her parents more time to get here, she heard the hushed tones of adults whispering to one another nearby. She didn't know why, but Clara was intrigued by them and felt an intense need to watch. The tones of their voices were urgent, fraught and low. Had there been a problem with a prop or some other aspect of the production? If so, Clara thanked her lucky stars; that would give her parents a chance to arrive and see her at her proudest moment, and Mama would be so happy, and Papa would give her his bouquet, and Ferdy would complain, but that was alright, because they would go home and have hot chocolate and then Clara would go to bed and dream of nothing but Christmas and dancing sugarplums.

One of the teachers glanced at her, followed by the other, and Clara felt her heart quicken. Was she in trouble? Had she done something wrong? Were they not letting her be the sugarplum fairy anymore? Clara's legs trembled and she threatened to fall to the floor in despair. No, not that, nothing was worse than that, they couldn't, they wouldn't, she had worked so hard and trained so well and...

One of the teachers came and tapped her on the shoulder.

"Clara, sweetie, I need you to come with me."

"No, I can't. I'm on stage in a minute." the girl said stubbornly. If they were going to give her part to someone else, then they would have to drag her away kicking and screaming.

"None of that matters now darling." explained the teacher cryptically. "Something... something bad has happened and I need you to be brave and come with me."

There was a tremble in her voice, and when Clara looked up she saw that the dance teacher's eyes were grave and shining with unshed tears. When she saw that, Clara realised that whatever she had to say in her defence, it was too late now. There was no going back.

Clara felt as if she were stepping on ice as she took her teacher's hand, and the woman led her away from the stage and down the corridor, into the main body of the school. Briefly, Clara thought they might be headed back into the changing room so that she could put on her normal clothes and bestow the fabulous tutu on whoever had replaced her, but her teacher just kept on walking. She was walking right to the entrance of the school.

At the side of the main door there was a small waiting room, the kind that had blinds on its window so you couldn't see outside or in. The taffeta on Clara's costume began to itch unbearably, and she shifted uncomfortably, a nervous sweat prickling at her armpits.

The door to the reception room opened. Behind the desk sat the secretary, and her eyes were glistening as she dabbed at them with the back of her hand.

And there, sat on a chair on the other side of the room, her hair mussed and her blotchy red face stained with tears as if she had been crying unbearably hard, was her mother.

"Mama?" asked Clara quizzically. "What's wrong? Where's Papa? You're about to miss my part in the show."

She didn't get the chance to say anything else before her mother shot up and crushed her into an enveloping hug, sobbing into her shoulder.

Back in The Fortress of Forgotten Things, Clara wiped away her own tears. Her father had never got to see her in the tutu that she now held in her hands, that was now stained with the essence of a memory so painful that it threatened to crush her. He'd never got to see it because, that evening, on his way home, another motorist had slammed sideways into him at a junction, and he'd died, cold and alone and away from those he loved, at age forty-two.

Clara couldn't hold it in anymore. She buried her face in the tutu and screamed and wept into its fabric; big guttural noises imbued with grief she'd been keeping a lid on for far too long.

She did this for a few minutes, and then pulled the garment away from her face and looked at it. Then, without really thinking about what she was doing, she imagined the child-sized tutu growing and changing, and the ballet slippers too; the entire ensemble becoming taller and longer until it no longer fit a scared little girl but a determined young woman. Next, she imagined that she herself was wearing what she had just created; that the tutu fitted like a glove in all the right places, and that the slippers flew swiftly to her feet and tied themselves neatly around her calves as if she had never worn another pair of shoes in her life. And then she imagined herself, looking exactly the way she had done that night, with her hair flowing in soft ringlets down to her shoulders and her face dewy and shiny with the makeup that was ready to sparkle under the stage lights, reflecting her beauty and making her a princess.

It was the amazed gasps from Shiverfinger and Bertram that brought her back to the present. Gingerly, Clara opened her eyes, looked down, and saw that she was indeed now wearing the tutu. On her feet were the satin slippers. She cast a glance at her shoulders and saw that her hair cascaded down in soft ringlets. There was a slight thud as the nutcracker fell to the ground, freed from her coat, which had now vanished.

Everything in her imagination had come to pass. She was The Sugarplum Fairy.

"Clara, you look amazing!" whispered Bertram softly.

She grinned at him, and then looked towards Shiverfinger.

"Pretty fairy." he said knowingly, and grinned.

"Pretty fairy." Clara agreed, finally understanding.

Suddenly a winter wind came blowing past them, and although it was fierce and sharp, Clara was sure she could hear something riding on its current; something that wasn't its howl.

"Can you hear that?" she asked her friends.

"What?" Bertram was puzzled.

Clara strained her hearing, listening intently to the gale. There was definitely something there.

"Clara, we need to go! If we don't hurry, The Mouse King will catch us!" warned Bertram.

"Just a moment." Clara told him distractedly.

All of a sudden, the wind changed direction and swirled around her in a ballet all of its own, and though it was filled with flecks of snow and ice, it did not hurt Clara or sting her body, but embraced her, and as the gust filled her ears, that was when she heard it, and fully understood.

Music.

But it was not just any music. It was the music that had been playing, all those years ago, when she had trained for months and months for the part her father had never got to see her play. It was the music that had been playing earlier that night – could it really have only been earlier that night? – when her mother had ordered her to perform in front of the party guests.

Clara heard the music and remembered: remembered a time long-since past. A time where dancing had not been a painful memory, but her life, something she ate, slept and breathed and loved with all that she had. She had been denying her soul for so long, and kept it submerged under her grief. The music took her back to happier times; the times when her father was alive, and when, if she had ever cried out for him, he had not been a ghost but instead a flesh-and-blood man, who came running to reassure her that it was just a little scratch or a bad dream and that nothing could ever harm her, not as long as he was there.

The music took her back to her heart's delight.

Without any word to Shiverfinger or Bertram, Clara stepped forward into the whirlwind that carried the music... and she danced. She danced the steps she had never danced on that horrible, fateful night, the steps that she had always felt tragedy had robbed her of, the steps she had always remembered even after all this time, because in her heart – her dancer's heart – she knew that it was impossible for her to forget the steps to a routine that had made a mark on her soul. She danced furiously, moving from one position to the next at a devilish pace; not with the graceful movements of a ballet dancer but with the frenzied movements of a person possessed. There was no beauty, only rage and determination, and as the whirlwind spun Clara around and around she answered it with an exhilarating series of dizzying pirouettes, and did not stop even when Bertram shouted her name and the world went white.

CHAPTER THIRTEEN
THE TRUTH

When Clara opened her eyes, she was not where she had been a few moments ago. Instead, she had fallen to the ground, exhausted from her dancing. The wind had vanished.

In the delicate outfit of The Sugarplum Fairy, she got to her feet and pushed herself upright. Blinking like a baby owlet, she looked around.

Green grass, as green as peppermints, stretched as far as the eye could see, and was dotted with wildflowers the colour of jewels that waved their stems lazily in the mild, warm breeze. The sky was the hazy blue of an August afternoon, with white fluffy clouds ambling across it. Trees, full with leaves the colour of emeralds, shone on their branches. And the birds! The birds made such music that they became an orchestra, twittering their symphonies with melodic notes that were filled with joy and jubilation. If she listened carefully over the sound of the birds however, Clara was sure she could hear the sound of whispering waves somewhere in the background too.

This was The Land of Light. She had made it.

Clara was filled with happiness at the thought, and she let out a little delighted laugh as a bird alighted on a nearby branch, a worm wriggling animatedly in its mouth. She was so enthralled that it took her a moment or two to realise there was something off about the creature.

It was not clad in feathers as it should have been, but was rather completely smooth, and pale pink in colour, with only slight lines on its abdomen to give the indication of wings. Its legs were too skinny and its eyes were too beady, and its beak was not a perfect point; rather, it had a little nodule on the end of it. Now she looked at it, the worm in its mouth was strange too; brown and green and blue, not pink like an earthworm should be. Was it... gummy?

A first glance left Clara unsure, but then she looked again and determined that she was right: everything here was made out of sweets.

She could see it now: the worm was indeed made from jelly, and the bird was made from sugar paste, its features piped on in chocolate icing. She looked up, past the bird, and now saw that the trunk of the tree was made from chocolate too, and its leaves were lime lollipops, their green sticks masquerading as their stems. The puffy clouds in the sky were soft shades of pink, lilac and peach – exactly the same shades as candyfloss – and now that she thought about it, there actually was a distinctly peppermint smell coming from the grass. With a smile, Clara turned away from the sugar bird and carried on walking.

It wasn't long until she came to a small park of sorts. A pathway made from white sprinkle-covered chocolate buttons trailed away into the distance, curving around a sparkling fountain that had been carved exquisitely from marzipan, which glistened in the sun. Water from it arched delicately into the air, and as it rose several feet Clara dashed over to it and caught some in her cupped hands. Putting it to her lips, she was surprised to learn that it was not water but in fact bubbling lemonade, sharp and refreshing on her tongue. Placed around the fountains were seats and benches made from

shaped candy cane and liquorice, and Clara sat
on one as she looked out to the horizon, past the
trees with their lollipop leaves, and mulled over
where she had found herself.

Clara marvelled at the beauty that
surrounded her. It was truly a paradise, an
infinite paradise that surpassed all her
expectations of what Heaven might have been
like. It was everything and more, so much more.

And yet, once again, her Papa was not
here.

She tried to quash the wave of grief that
reawakened inside of her. She had always known
that this would be a distinct possibility of course,
but all the way through her adventure, her new
friends had sworn that this would be the place

that contained her heart's delight, where he would be waiting to embrace her again, but he was not. She was alone.

Just as she was beginning to wonder how she would ever make it home, something started to quiver out of the corner of her eye. She turned to the motion and, with slowly-dawning horror, realised what the object was. She picked it up from where it lay, trembling, on the ground.

It was the nutcracker. It must have got caught up in the tempest that brought her here! Now, the strange little figure was opening, vibrating in her hand with so much energy that it rattled out of her grasp and, as Clara shrieked in surprise, fell to the floor. The nutcracker became a blur in its agitated movements, and Clara was sure it was about to burst.

Suddenly, there was a brilliant flash. Clara was temporarily blinded, and she threw her hand to her face to shield her eyes. After a few moments the light receded, and she gradually regained her vision and looked at the place where the nutcracker had been. What she found left her breathless. Instead of a doll, there was now a man, dressed in a smart black tuxedo, his dark hair smoothed back so that he looked like a handsome prince.

And then he turned, and Clara's heart stopped.

The nutcracker prince was her father.

He stared at her with the soulful eyes that had stared out at her from the painting in his study, and they twinkled with an unmistakeable vivacity only he possessed. His handlebar moustache was styled in the way it always had been, and his face was filled with his characteristic warmth.

"Clara?" he whispered carefully, as if there was a spell cast over them that he dared not break.

The girl was dumbfounded. It was her Papa's voice, coming out of a man who looked unmistakeably like her Papa, and yet... it couldn't be.

"No." she murmured as quietly as he had. She took a step back. "No. I... I saw you, at the funeral..."

"Clara, my sugarplum fairy." he said suddenly; he was louder now, more authoritative in his tone. "It's me."

At that last simple statement, any reserve Clara had dissolved and, tears blinding her, she rushed to her Papa and crushed him to her. His arms came around her, and he kissed the top of her head soothingly.

"Sh, sh. It is alright." he consoled over the sound of her sobbing.

"I just can't believe it's you." she said, withdrawing from his embrace and wiping her eyes.

"And I can't believe it is you!" he said admiringly, his voice full of pride. "My little girl. All grown up."

Her face broke into a grin. "How are you here?"

"I will tell you all that shortly, for although you must hear what it is I have to say, we must first make things right between us." He sighed regretfully. "Clara, the night I died, I was on my way to see you dance. I had stopped off at the florist's to get a bouquet for you as I always did; I was so excited to see you perform! But I never got there."

"Another car ran into you." Clara said quickly. She had heard the circumstances surrounding her father's death many times, and had no wish to go over it again.

Nicklaus nodded sagely. "Yes. It was bad weather though, with a lot of rain; it was not the other driver's fault. I have forgiven him his mistake. What was unforgiveable was what happened next." he said bitterly. Then he shook his head. "I never got to see you dance, my darling. You never got to see my pride." He got down on one knee, in his scarlet soldier's uniform, and held his hand out to her in an old fashioned gesture of respect. "Would you dance with me now? To make things right?"

Before Clara could reply, she heard the birds loudly change their tune; they were now whistling the song that had brought her here, the one that was engraved into her memory. "Yes." she told her Papa, her voice cracking with emotion that she could barely conceal.

And so they danced. They danced the routine that Clara had remembered all this time, the dance that her Papa should have seen eight years ago, but never did. She was surprised that he could dance as well as he did, for he was so sure and swift-of-foot that he matched Clara exactly, and she was tall and confident beside him. No longer was she a little girl standing on her father's toes but his equal in elegance and poise as he lifted her and twirled her in his embrace. Originally, in the concept of the ballet, the dance was meant to be romantic, but partnered with her father it became a dance of a very different kind of love; a love that was paternal, familial, forever.

As Clara finished the last step, she and Papa bowed to each other with a flourish. As they raised their lowered heads, they smiled at one another. Suddenly, her father cast a worried glance at the sky, and Clara saw that it was no longer the warm afternoon but dusky twilight, the sun sinking low behind the fondant hills.

"We don't have much time left." Nicklaus said sadly. "Please... walk with me. There's something you need to know."

Looking at him concernedly, Clara linked his arm through his, and they meandered down the chocolate button path until the sea came into view; a sea that was also lemonade, like the water in the fountains had been.

"Clara, what I am about to tell you will be very difficult to take in, but you must listen." Papa urged.

"Of course."

"When we die, our bodies cease to exist on the Plane we were born in, but our souls are eternal. We travel here, to The Land of Light."

"Ye- wait a minute. How do you know that this is called The Land of Light? How do you know about Planes?"

He smiled at her crookedly. "I've learnt a lot in my years as a ghost. Besides, I was with you when you spoke to Father Winter."

Clara looked at him, confused. He smiled at her, holding her gaze, waiting for her to come to some kind of realisation, but she couldn't fathom how what he had said made sense.

And then she thought.

She thought about Uncle Drosselmeyer giving her the nutcracker, and telling her how precious it was to him.

She thought about her gut instinct to carry the nutcracker with her everywhere she went, despite finding it creepy and unsettling.

She thought about her utmost refusal to give the nutcracker to The Mouse King, even though it would have guaranteed her freedom.

The nutcracker.

"You were there the whole time!" Clara exclaimed.

Nicklaus nodded. "Yes. And it has been my heart's delight travelling with you, Clara, for you have developed into a kind, brave and wise young woman. I could not be prouder of you."

We had quite an adventure, didn't we?" said Clara warmly.

"We did." agreed Nicklaus.

"But how did you get inside the nutcracker in the first place?"

Her father's look darkened. "I had died and was ready to join The Land of Light. It is the natural order of things that a person's spirit must go free once they have passed. But someone used dark arts to bind me to our Plane, so that I could never leave. They took scraps of my clothes and possessions and used an unspeakable alchemy to seal me inside the nutcracker. I've been trapped inside that figure for eight years like a prisoner. I should be free, Clara! I am only here now because you wish it to be; the dark magic is too powerful to allow me to stay of my own volition, but how I long to! I would never do anything to hurt you, you know that, but I died, and no matter how much my loved ones might miss me, my soul longs to go. Clara, my darling, you have to set me free. Say you will set me free."

"But who would do such a thing?" Clara was incredulous. "Who would entrap you like that? I don't know anyone who has the power!"

The gaze of her Papa was steady as he said: "Uncle Drosselmeyer."

Clara gaped at him, unable to believe what she was hearing. Suddenly, there was a mighty commotion, as if from afar; yelling voices and angry shouts coming rapidly closer.

"The Mouse King!" Clara cried, her voice full of pain and panic.

Nicklaus smiled at her. "It is time for you to go home now, my daughter. Tell your mother and brother I love them very much. But above all, promise you will set me free."

"Wait, Papa!" The sounds of the mouse legion were advancing at a steady pace now, becoming louder than even the chorus of the birds. "The Mouse King... he said he wanted the nutcracker, he wanted what was inside it. But how did he know? Why would he want you?"

Her father took her by the forearms.

"Clara... when you were in Mausburg and negotiating with The Mouse King, he said your name."

"Yeah, so?"

"You had never given it to him."

Clara fell silent as she thought back.

I know others have a tendency to paint me and the mice as cold-blooded killers, but the reality is that I rule my kingdom firmly and justly. I'm not a bad person Clara. Just... misunderstood.

Her father was right. She had never told The Mouse King her name, and yet he had known it. Her face went white.

"What does this mean? That Uncle Drosselmeyer and The Mouse King know each other? Did Uncle Drosselmeyer promise The Mouse King something if he could make you come back? Are they in league with one another? How could that be?" her mind whirled, and she had to shout now; the mice were coming closer, coming to rip her out of The Land of Light...

Her Papa chuckled sadly. "Clara... Uncle Drosselmeyer is The Mouse King."

CHAPTER FOURTEEN
ALL MADE RIGHT

Clara sat bolt upright with a gasp, the soft fabric of her father's chair enveloping her. From further down the hall, she could hear the sound of Christmas carols and soft chatter. The skirts of her party dress ruffled as she looked around, bewildered.

She was home.

She stood up out of the Chesterfield, and as she did, something clattered to the ground. Looking down, she saw her uncle's nutcracker grinning up at her. Slowly, she bent and retrieved it. Holding the figure to her chest, she furiously marched out of the door and into the corridor.

She barged past the guests, ignoring their curious looks as she did so, and made it to the grand hallway. The place was still teeming with people, but that didn't stop her from hearing the clocks striking twelve. Nor did it stop her from seeing exactly who she was looking for trying to slink away from the party like a sly rodent.

"Uncle!" she called.

Her voice was so loud that all the guests in the room stopped talking and turned to look between her and Drosselmeyer.

"Clara." Uncle Drosselmeyer's voice was as smooth as silk, yet his eyes kept darting for an escape route. Clara recognised the voice of The Mouse King immediately. "I am so glad you like your present."

"You monster." Clara growled. Her voice was full of fury and her eyes filled with unshed tears.

"Clara, I meant what I said to you. I am not a tyrant."

"Tell that to my father!"

The noise of their argument had now attracted the attention of her mother and Ferdy, who crossed the room with worried faces. "What's going on?" asked Mama as she stood behind her daughter and put a protective hand on her shoulder.

"Our uncle trapped Papa's soul in this after he died and now he can't be free." Clara said as she showed her the nutcracker. "We have to let him go."

"What?" whispered Pyotr from his position in the corner, where he held a tray of canapés. "The master is in there?"

"I'm afraid so, Pyotr." Clara spat, never taking her eyes from Uncle Drosselmeyer's rapidly-reddening face. "I'm sorry that you have to hear the truth like this."

"Clara, don't be so ridiculous! It is ridiculous!" cried Mama. When Drosselmeyer didn't concur, she turned to face him. "Isn't it? You were always into some strange things, old man..."

The conniving wizard floundered under the sharp gaze of his niece-in-law. "I did it for us. So we could keep him with us, forever!"

Clara stepped forward, bravely. "And what about all those people in The Hinterworld? Bertram, Father Winter, and the flower fae?" she asked him in a low voice only he could hear. "Were they for us, too?" When he failed to answer her, she nodded with bitter acknowledgement. "I thought so. Tyrant." She turned away from him and went back to her family. "It's time my father went to The Land of Light."

"No!" Drosselmeyer shrieked, and with surprising strength he slammed his walking stick straight into the ground. Ice shot out from it and

encircled Clara's feet, freezing her to the spot
where she stood, and she groaned and protested
as the doors and windows banged open with the
force of dark magic. The party guests screamed
and cowered as Drosselmeyer, now straight-
backed and proud, walked up to Clara and
gloated down at her as she struggled.

"Such a brave little sugarplum fairy." he
sneered. "All she wants to do is send her Papa to
The Land of Light, so he can have his heart's
truest delight! Well, I won't let her. He might
have been her father, but he was my nephew! I
loved him like a son! I found a way to enter The
Hinterworld without the curse! He could have
ruled beside me as a prince! She was only meant
to be the key! But no... now she wants to let him

go, but I'll freeze them all in ice before they take him from me!"

Just at that moment, Clara was distracted by a sharp squeak that came from the left of her. She turned, and saw a mouse on his hind legs, looking at her with kind, inquisitive eyes, his whiskers twitching.

And he was wearing a red waistcoat.

He looked at her. She looked at him. Far away, in the distance, Clara heard something that might have been the wind... or the growl of a great bear. She smiled.

"You can't Drosselmeyer. After all, there's only one man who controls the winter around here."

At that exact moment, the front door blew open, slamming back on its hinges, and Clara's icy shackles shattered as a gust of wind roared into the room and swept Drosselmeyer up. The man screamed at its ferocity, but the storm would not relent. It shook him from side to side, as if he were a ragdoll caught in the mouth of some great beast. Then, with surprising strength, another finger of wind swept in and carried him right to the ceiling; so delicate was it that it got in between the crystals in the chandelier and made them tinkle like laughter. From her vantage point on the ground, Clara could see Drosselmeyer slowly beginning to freeze, with crystals forming on his eyelashes and nose. When the wind finally released him to the ground, he was almost completely frozen, and he could do nothing but stare at Clara with eyes filled with resentment as the fractals crept over his body and turned his face white as he solidified. Then, in a jarring contrast, a warm breeze swept into the room; a breeze that carried the scent of daffodils and roses, and it swirled around the wintry statue of Drosselmeyer, melting it until all that was left of him was a damp, pale puddle that one might find after a spring thaw.

Clara let out a sigh of relief and nodded her thanks at the unseen forces before they left just as quickly as they had arrived, closing the windows and doors and making the house warm again.

She grinned. It was all over.

Well, almost.

"Nicklaus?" She heard her mother whisper to the nutcracker that she cradled in her arms, having rescued it from the devastation caused by Drosselmeyer's demise. Ferdy stood next to her, his arm wrapped around her shoulders. She looked at Clara with hopeful eyes.

Clara shook her head. "He can't answer you Mama. He's stuck in there."

Mary sighed. "Then I suppose we really have got to let him go. But... how do we do it?"

Clara said nothing. Instead, she gently took the nutcracker from her mother, laid it softly down on the floor and murmured:

"Into time's depths I have now delved,
And made the clocks start at the stroke of
twelve.
I went into The Land of Light,
To make things right with my heart's delight.
A tyrant has now been defeated,
Cruelty and vanity have been unseated.
So now I set my loved one free,
As Sugarplum Fairy, this I decree."

The nutcracker started to tremble again, as it had done in The Land of Light, and Clara motioned for her family to step back. The flash blinded them, and Clara turned away and only looked back again once she heard the surprised gasps of the guests and her mother's shocked scream.

"Nicklaus!"

There, in front of them, was the shimmering apparition of her father, looking as noble as he had in life.

"Papa?" whispered Ferdy.

The ghost nodded and smiled at him, then drifted over towards Mama and tenderly cupped her cheek. She leaned into his hand and closed her eyes, tears leaking out from under her lids. Nothing needed to be said.

Lastly, he turned to Clara, and the pair exchanged a knowing glance.

"Go." she told him kindly.

Looking round at his family, Nicklaus Stahlbaum smiled at them one last time. Then, with their arms wrapped around each other,

Clara, Ferdy and their Mama watched as the spirit turned his back, walked through the closed window, and ascended into the starlit night to become part of the Kingdom of Heaven, forever.

CHAPTER FIFTEEN
NEW BEGINNINGS

The snow was melting and wet on the branches of the nearby trees as the train pulled into the station. Clara, carrying all her luggage, made sure she was the first to board, especially since she was carrying a cup of hot chocolate.

She reached the carriage and easily selected a seat on the back row as others made a fuss of where to sit. Settling down, Clara put her hot chocolate on the little table in front of her and rummaged in her suitcase for her cardigan.

She found it, and bumped into her new pair of ballet slippers as she did. Clara grinned upon seeing them. After all this hard work, she couldn't give up her Geography degree, but she could certainly join the city's ballet school that was just down the road from the university and try to become the best ballerina that the world had ever seen.

Feeling thrilled at the prospect of new adventures, Clara sat back, popped in her headphones, and waited for the train to take her towards the horizon.

And if anyone noticed the little brown mouse wearing a red waistcoat that peeped out and smiled at her from the collar of her jumper, they chose not to mention it.

ACKNOWLEDGMENTS

Writing a book at a time when there was also a
global pandemic was not an easy task. I wrote *On
the Stroke of Twelve* almost in secrecy, being
isolated and at home for an extended period of
time. That being said, it does not mean that there
were not people who did not help me when I
needed it.

Firstly I would like to thank my mother
for supplying me with motivation, and Simon for
supplying me with gin.

Special thanks go to my uncle, Iain Barker, who, as an author himself, provided solidarity and a sympathetic ear, despite a period of personal struggle that would make a lesser man quake. I am so proud of you.

To my beloved Granny Joan – you finally got your next book! Thank you for always seeing the best in me.

Martin; thank you for always being my proof-reader and always assuring me that I am a good writer, even when I don't feel like it.

I would like to extend my gratitude to my Facebook family, particularly Joey, who coined the term 'Paraplegionaire' and is waiting very patiently for his sequel (which I swear is coming next – you now have that in writing).

Thank you to Natalie Goes and my cousin, Justin Emery, for helping me with the German translations.

I would also like to give a big – albeit belated – round of applause to the cast of The New York City Ballet's 2011 performance of *The Nutcracker,* which was posted onto YouTube by the company and was pivotal to obtaining a deeper understanding of my source material.

And lastly, I would like to extend my warmest thanks to all those who have worked hard, stayed inside and just kept going through all the long months of this unprecedented year. As a disabled woman, nothing is more magical to me than ballet; the elegance and the grace that people somehow manage to convey with their feet. I hope that this book brings some magic to you.

Printed in Great Britain
by Amazon